I'm an Extra Character... Right?

M. S. CRYSTAL

RoseDog Books

PITTSBURGH, PENNSYLVANIA 15238

RoseDog Books
585 Alpha Drive
Suite 103
Pittsburgh, PA 15238
Visit our website at *www.rosedogbookstore.com*

ISBN: 979-8-89211-123-2
eISBN: 979-8-89211-621-3

I'm an Extra Character... Right?

Dedication for my parents and my sisters, who always supported and encouraged me to follow my dreams.

Prologue

All my life, for as long as I can remember, I've been totally normal. My childhood was ordinary, I had friends, I had tastes that I knew would change over time, and dreams that I knew were just that, dreams, they are things of life, right?

Yes, I admit that I am part of the girls who expected an old woman to knock on the door saying "Hello, I am a queen and you are my granddaughter, next successor to the throne." Okay, that's already an exaggeration.

I didn't expect anything big to happen in my life, no drastic change. Like every person, I expected my life to be normal, just with my small life achievements.

Chapter 1

JASMINE

Like every morning, I woke up to the music that my mom plays on Saturdays. I rub my eyes and take my phone, I check if there is any notification but no, nothing, just an ad that says I was selected to win a million dollars.

HA! I wish that was real.

I completely get out of bed, grab a pair of pants and a shirt, and head to the bathroom. I relieve myself, change and leave the room. I pass the rooms of my parents and my sister, I arrive at the kitchen, where my mother is.

"*Hola mija*, until you wake up" my mom said while heating tortillas.

Yawning, I told her. "*Ma'* it's nine in the morning and it's Saturday, you don't need to wake up early."

"For me it doesn't matter what day it is, you wake up because you do. *Punto.*" I approach and greet her with a kiss on the cheek.

I didn't look at my dad anywhere so I asked my mom. "Where is my dad?" I took a banana and ate it.

"In the backyard."

I leave the kitchen and go to the patio, I look for him and find him putting cement in the yard. I go back into the kitchen to serve a glass of water and take it to him, he realizes that I am approaching him and he gets up.

"*Mirate nomas que greñuda andas.*"

"Good morning dad."

He accepts the glass of water and drinks it.

I let him do his things and I go back to the room, I see myself in the mirror and see that my hair is a mess. I grab the brush and braid myself. Since today is Saturday, it is possible that either one of the neighbors comes to see my mom or I will have to go to the grocery store with my mom. Whenever one of the ladies comes over, it's just for pure gossip. In this neighborhood, if you want to know something, my mom's friends are the ones to know everything in detail.

I went back to my room also because I need to tidy up a bit, I have clothes everywhere.

"Jasmine, lend me your blue shirt!" my sister yelled.

"*Ni madres*, after a while you will not return it to me!" she does not answer but I hear her footsteps coming forward.

"Come on, I'll give it back to you."

"You said the same with my white tennis shoes but now, where are they?"

"I told you that the neighbor's *chucho* broke them."

"Yes, of course." I say sarcastically, I turn to arrange the things on the dresser and Vanessa leaves.

I finish tidying up the rest of the room and go to the living room, I turn on the TV but can't find anything to watch, all the channels have ads or news. At this time there are almost no movies. As I keep searching I hear the doorbell ring. I was going to get up to open it but heard my mom approaching.

I see my mom almost run to the door. "Coming!" she said and seconds later I hear that 'ladies scream'.

"*Hola comadre*, how are you?" Both greet each other and enter the living room.

And so ladies and gentlemen, start with the morning news, starting with a review of what happened last week and then what's new today! My mom gets up and makes coffee. I get out of there because that particular lady always asks for me but I know that it is because she wants to introduce me to her son and it is that she almost managed to convince my mother that we have dinner with both families so we can get to know each other.

Lady, watching novelas is not in vain.

My phone began to ring and I looked at the screen to see who it was, I smiled and answered immediately.

"Hi girl."

So I stayed talking with my cousin on the phone. After talking to her for an hour, and a few scolding from my mom for talking loud and laughing like a seal, I went to the kitchen to find something to eat, looked at an apple and grabbed it.

"But listen to me, don't get too close with that woman," says my mom's friend with a slightly serious tone. "Because she herself told me that her son had just been released from prison and God knows why he was there from the beginning." my mom covers her mouth with shock, I just roll my eyes.

It surprises me how much both women are surprised by everything they say to each other, they feel that every bad thing that happens in this place is because of the devil—It can be said that both are very religious, very—I don't know how much time passed until the lady left, then my mom started cooking. I look at the clock on the wall, it's noon.

How these women talk, and me without doing something productive.

Later my dad comes in and helps my mom prepare some stuff for dinner, I've always seen how my parents have a relationship, with balance and demonstrations that only they understand and it's something I'd like to experience but I guess it won't be soon, I'm almost halfway through year of finishing the last year of high school. and I haven't been through that 'teenage romance' that everyone talks about. Sometimes yes, I would like but not in this time- life.

We all ate quietly, my sister spent the time talking about something that happened in one of her classes, my mom listening to her and my dad focusing on his food, the same as me. At the end we all went to do our thing, I went to my room.

I go to bed staring at the ceiling, thinking how 'interesting' my life is... nothing comes to mind. I am a teenager—okay an adult—of 19 years, sometimes I work, I have a few friends and a "best friend"; I came to like someone but they only stayed in the depths of my mind, I never really confessed and, honestly, it scared me and I just kept thinking *"what if...?"*. A slow torture.

Tomorrow is Sunday and I'll probably go to the mall with my mom, or just go to the store quickly to get some snacks. I took my pajamas and I went to take a bath. When I got out of the bathroom I went back to bed and decided to stay up late watching a movie, one that I know will make me wonder why I don't do something interesting in my life, should I get a tattoo? Do I dye my hair? Maybe a piercing?

Nah, my mom would kill me if I do some of those things.

The movie is already halfway through but I'm not paying attention to it. Out of nowhere I remember what that lady told my mom, about that boy who just got out of prison, I think I came across him a few times. Whenever I saw him, he had a serious face.

At least, he does have something to talk about in his life. He can say something like, 'I was in prison but I don't want to talk about it' and proceed to act mysterious and more people will be interested in him, simply because they want to know why he was in that place.

I decide I have enough and settle down to sleep. I turned off the computer and fell asleep.

Chapter 2

JASMINE

I'll make a mental note about never letting my mom accompany me shopping for underwear, especially if I plan to go to Victoria's Secret, the fact that my mom is criticizing every item in that store, complaining about how 'inappropriate' they are, and she only says, "Well, who is she going to show it to or what?" I love my mom, I really do, but there are times when I would rather come to places without her.

"I just don't understand" and she continues.

"*Ya ma*', it is something that you are not going to use."

"Not even you *chamaca*! If I ever find you one of those *tangas* I swear you won't even tell."

"Don't worry, I won't." If she knew, I have two sets of lingerie but I bought them because they looked pretty but I feel ashamed to use them.

We left the mall and returned to the neighborhood but on the way, my mom saw one of her 'friends'. Just by seeing her I know that we will stay here for a long minute. It's not that it bothers me, I'm used to it, I can't tell her that I'll go to the house because she wouldn't let me. I just stayed there playing on my phone.

Out of nowhere I got a chill and the first thing I thought was that a ghost just passed by me.

If I keep watching videos about paranormal facts I will go crazy.

I looked around me out of pure curiosity and my sight stopped at a house that is half a block from here; a house that looked neglected but it seemed that there were people living there. The house is scary, I looked towards a window and I swear I paralyzed for a moment, maybe I hallucinated or it's because is from far away but seriously I saw a person being strangled, my mom took me by the shoulder and reacted, I turned to see her but I returned my gaze to the house but there was nothing.

"Let's go *mija*." says my mom, stealing my attention.

"Yeah…" I looked again but, nothing.

"What's wrong?" my mom asks me with a frown.

"Ah? Nothing, I just got distracted looking at that house." my mom looked at the house and went pale.

"Don't even stare at it, because that house is where that boy lives, the one who just got out of jail."

"Okay…" so that's where he lives.

The four of us are eating dinner, my mom and my sister are talking while my dad and I are watching TV; there are action movies tonight. In the background I can hear the wind, early, in the news they said that there would possibly be a storm.

I don't like storms.

Suddenly the light went out, by reflex, I made my hands into fists. A habit that I have had since I was a child, every time I get scared or have a strong emotion, I make my hands into fists.

"The storm is getting ugly, girls go to your room and close the windows. Be sure to put cans in if you have roof leaks." My mom gets up followed by my sister, me too, picking up my plate and taking it to the sink.

Entering my room I feel a presence, the window is open and the curtains are moving with force, the first thing I do is close the window, when I do so I immediately turn to see my room. I don't see anyone but feel so, I tried to ignore that feeling since I never liked storms, I guess that's it. I took a quick shower and changed. I have school tomorrow and don't want to look like a zombie, so I went to sleep.

I wake up hearing a loud sound, sit on my bed and look around, I see that the window is open... the window is open.

What the hell?! Why is it open?! I closed it!

I got up and went to close it, and make sure it didn't reopen. When I turned around I saw a dark shadow pass into my closet, I was frozen in my place. I was hoping this was just something my mind was creating; I didn't know whether to get close or not because in the movies they always kill the curious one.

If it's a scared cat that came for refuge? Yes, it can be, if it's a serial killer who is waiting for me to get close to kill me?... it can also be.

I did the most reasonable thing at this moment, I took my blanket and left the room and went to my sister's. I moved her a little if she was awake but she didn't make a sound. I closed the door and got into bed with her.

When her alarm went off, I got up and went back to my room. Being daylight it will be easier for me to investigate my closet. I opened it slowly and looked around, there was nothing, just my normal mess; I breathed a sigh of relief and put my hand on my chest, it was just my hallucinations. I took a sweater and closed the doors.

Ready, I left my room and went to the kitchen, where my mom was making breakfast.

When she saw me she told me, "Now come to eat." I sat at the table and that's what I did.

"Ma, did you come into my room last night?"

"No, why?"

"For nothing, just asking." Someone definitely opened that window, because the air was not that bad and it is not possible for it to open like that.

When I finished I left the house, it was already late. The walk to school is not very far, it only takes me about 20 minutes to walk—okay, 10 minutes but I'm lazy—I looked at the houses as I passed until I got to that house where I saw...

According to my mother, that lady lives there with her son, the one who got out of prison, what did he do? I don't know. I feel like just looking at that house I'm already doing something wrong. I kept walking and the closer I got, the colder it felt and it even started to get windy but there is still time until it is autumn.

I accelerated a little, I don't want to be late. Reaching the corner, before crossing, someone collided with me causing us both to fall to the ground.

"Watch where you're going!" Without looking at him I yelled at him, I scraped my knee and it hurts.

"Sorry!" he says and continues running.

And my stupid help? That bastard didn't even bother to help me up.

I hope they give him detention for being late, luckily my first class was with a teacher who liked me.I got up and brushed off my pants, I'm lucky that this school doesn't force us to wear a uniform because if I had a skirt right now, I'm sure that when I fell I would have been shown everything!

I arrived at school and went straight to my classroom. The first thing that happened was that my 'friend' saw me and she came towards me.

Chapter 3

JASMINE

Before my friend came over, she was talking to some of her other friends, she has always been popular with the students and teachers, she always stands out and is very friendly.

When she wants.

"Hi girl! How are you?"

"Good, sleepy but good and you?"

"I'm super good." She moves her hands while she talks, all good with that when people do it but she only does it with one purpose, she wants you to see something.

"I'm glad, and something new that you want to tell me?" I said it just to her to stop moving so exaggeratedly, she already fixed her hair like five times.

"Now that you ask, let me tell you yes! My dad gave me this beautiful bracelet." She raises her hand and bends her wrist, showing me the bracelet. "It's pretty, isn't it?"

"It is…"

She is Mindy, a girl of standard height, skinny, white skin and brown hair. Her father is a *gringo* but her mother is from England and that somehow makes her proud and sometimes she imitates the English accent but let's just say it sounds like a bad imitation of *Peppa pig*.

"Hey, a question, did you do your homework for calculus class? I didn't do it and I wanted to see if you could help me." I was going to answer but a boy who entered the classroom caught my attention. I had never seen him and he has a very... strange air. "Jasmine?"

"What?"

"Are you listening to me?"

"No, not really." I noticed how she blinked too much. I feel that she craves and desires attention like a drug because when the attention isn't on her, she becomes unbearable. "But I did do my homework if that's what you want." I said with a fake smile.

"I thank you from the bottom of my heart." I know you're lying to me.

The class went normally, Mindy sat next to me and sometimes talked to me but most of the time she talked to others, she was never satisfied with just talking to one person. The class ended and everyone went their way. I looked at how she left with a group of university students, the more "important" the better for her. As I started my way home I looked at that boy again. He was sitting in the shade of a tree looking in my direction, there were many students so he must have seen something interesting.

When I was home, my mom immediately put me to wash the dishes. My mom has that disorder that every Mexican mom has and it's called extreme cleanliness. I finished and went to my room but I felt something strange. I looked everywhere but there was nothing, at least nothing out of place.

I didn't wash my clothes? Is it colder? Didn't I pick up my room?

I ignored the feeling and lay down on the bed but got up immediately.

"What the..." I looked at the sheets carefully, there was dirt and some twigs, as if someone had stood on it with boots full of mud or something like that.

Something is definitely wrong.

I checked my room in more detail, there's nothing out of the ordinary but... maybe it's something I can't see, maybe feel? I'm going crazy, there shouldn't be something weird here. I looked at the closet again and remembered what I had thought I saw last night, I felt a chill run through my entire body. I look out the window, it's about to get dark.

I approached the closet doors, I had already checked it this morning and there was nothing but what if what I saw was something, a cat, right? I opened it and it was just my clothes and some shoes...just as it should be. I looked around once more and right in a corner there was something black stuck to the wall, it looked like something slimy but I don't want to touch it.

An old candy? Mold? Mud?

I left my room and went for a rag and a broom, when I returned that stain was gone, I dropped the broom and immediately put my hand around my neck, taking my pulse. I'm fine, my pulse is a little high, but I'm going crazy!

Have I drugged myself without realizing it? No, if so, why would I be seeing creepy things and not the unicorn that should give me money.

I look again but there is nothing. I took my phone and turned on the lamp, looked where the stain was supposed to be and it was immediately cleaned... It was cleaned. I didn't want to get scared, there has to be an explanation for this, ghosts? I don't think so, I do believe in those things but there would be no reason to come and scare me, I haven't done anything.

I was in the living room talking to Mindy, she called me with the excuse that she wanted to know if I already studied for the exams that were coming up, but I decided to talk to her about what I saw.

"Are you sure that's what you saw?"

"Yes, I don't know what it was but it looked slimy."

"That's scary..." things were heard on the other side of the line, it seemed that there were more people with her. "Where is the popcorn?... look in the upper cabinet."

"If you are busy, you can hang up." I knew that she was not calling me just to find out about the exams, she surely wanted me to know that there were people with her.

"They are friends from the university, I didn't invite you because I know you don't know anyone and I thought you wouldn't have fun." Yeah, sure. I still wonder how Mindy has friends who are from college if she hasn't finished high school yet.

"Sure, well, see you, bye." She didn't say goodbye and hung up.

I stared at the screen, I know that she is somehow popular at school and it's not something that interests me but I wanted to have someone to talk to, I don't know why she decided to talk to me in the first place. Since I entered high school I didn't have many of friends I only talked to others about work or homework but I didn't go out with them or talk to them outside of school, in my third year Mindy decided to talk to me and I felt happy, but I quickly realized that she only did it out of interest and for more attention.

I know my life is calm and I don't have anecdotes to tell, it's "normal" but I have a hobby that makes me realize that my life is boring, without emotion or even something interesting, books give me dreams that I knew they won't come true, a hot guy will not come to my door saying "you are the love of my life and I only have eyes for you".

I left my phone on the couch and went to get some money, I wanted some *pan dulce* and there wasn't any at home so I decided to go to the store. I went out and tried to walk quickly because it's almost night. I had to go by that house but I didn't want to, I'd be afraid to go there after I thought I saw someone being murdered. I have enough with the scare I gave myself today.

When I got to the store, there were only a few people. I went to where the bread was and grabbed a bag, I put a few and then I went for a juice. I approached the cashier.

"Hello," I greeted and the old lady greeted me with a smile.

While she was scanning things, I felt someone approaching from behind, like a buyer… maybe. I stepped aside, out of courtesy, and he approached; he is a man dressed in black, he even has a black mask. His presence gave me chills.

"It will be $10.25" I took out my wallet and gave her my card.

That man was just standing there without saying anything and I don't know whether to feel calm or nervous. But for some reason we don't talk more than we are supposed to.

"It's too late at night for someone to be out."

Chapter 4

JASMINE

"I'm sorry?"

"It's too late at night for someone to go out." I looked at him confused, well he's out too.

"I would say the same but I have no interest in other people's affairs." I think I was a bit rude, I heard how he laughed a little.

"Of course, my apologies." He sounded like a guy of no more than 25 years old.

"No, forgive me, I shouldn't have answered like that." The lady returned my card and took my bag. "Well, bye, have a good night."

"You too."

I left the store and continued on my way. Well, he was strange, I didn't recognize him or anything, and I suppose he didn't go to school because he seemed older. I got home and the first thing I did was pour myself a glass of milk and then go to my room. The week has just started and I'm still in school-time, but I really don't want to go to bed early today.

I ended up eating bread and then I fell asleep.

The alarm went off and I woke up, I changed and went out, I looked at the clock, it's earlier than normal. I think I fixed myself faster or I set the alarms early, I don't know. I decided to go to school but not before leaving a note telling my mom that I already left; the street is lonelier than normal, passing by the house of fear—that's how I nicknamed it— I saw that there was something different, there was an armchair with a blanket, as if someone had been there a few minutes ago.

The door was flung open revealing two people arguing.

"You're an idiot! Don't you think? You just got out of the damn prison!" She was a very angry woman.

"As if that mattered to you! You never went to visit me, you never went to fucking see me once!"

"I was taking care of your father, you don't see that he is sick!"

"Sick?! You call that being sick? He is a fucking drunk who does nothing but make our lives miserable!"

"If you hate this life so much, get the hell out of here!"

This is really uncomfortable, I shouldn't be listening. I almost ran to get past that house. When I arrived at the school, there were almost no students. I entered and went to the cafeteria; the breakfast here is passable so I went to grab some cereal and a banana. I went to sit at a table, while looking around me, there were very few students. I ended up looking at the guy I had seen yesterday, it seems to me that he is a new student. I decided to concentrate on my food.

"Hello." I looked up and looked at him, he was in front of my table.

"Hello…"

"Can I sit?" I was going to say no because I still remember him bumping into me and causing me to scrape myself but I decided not to say that.

"Yeah, sure." And that he did, he sat in front of me, now I feel uncomfortable.

"I'm new here and I don't really know anyone and well, I hope you don't mind me sitting next to you."

"Don't worry, I understand." So yes, I was right.

During the whole time no one spoke, we just accompanied each other, when the bell rang we both got up and each one went on our own. I arrived at my room and I was surprised to see that Mindy was not there, she almost never missed class, well at least today it will be calm.

It's lunch time but I don't eat at school. I left and went to a store to buy something, some students were given permission to go out and I am from that group. When I got there, I grabbed a sandwich and a peach juice.

Should I grab some cookies for later?

While I was deciding someone stood in front of me, I looked up and saw that guy from last night. We stared at each other and I don't know why but we both laughed.

"Would it be something usual to see us in stores?"

"I don't know." I didn't even know his name and I didn't know his face, he was wearing his mask.

"Okay." He says with a mocking tone. "What's your name?"

"Jasmine, you?"

"Thiago" Well, now I know.

"Well I need to go back to school." I smiled at him as a farewell, I went to the cashier and left.

Thiago. It is a nice name.

The rest of the school was fine, I ran into that mysterious boy a few times but we didn't speak, just a look and a nod. At the start, as always, I went home. While I was walking—I was already close to the house of fear—I saw someone leave the house, he was putting on his mask and turned to my direction and stopped.

So he's the same guy from the store.

I don't know why but I felt as if I shouldn't have known who he was, not too soon at least. I feel that he's wearing that mask for some reason... wait a minute... I forgot the fact that he's the same one who just came out of the bars. Out of inertia I took a step back, but my house is forward so whether I wanted to or not I had to go forward. He finished walking down the front steps and looked at me a little doubtful.

"Hi, um…" I could tell that he was uncomfortable.

"I'll be honest, okay, I'm not one to judge people, I don't have the right to do that, so whatever you did has nothing to do with me." Then I just went on my way.

Everyone in this neighborhood knows that the boy who just got out of prison lives in that house and whoever they see coming out of that house can easily find out who he was. I know maybe I'll avoid him every time I see him but only because I know I'll get nervous. I don't know what he did but it was surely something serious because in the situation there are only people who did very bad things.

I am in my bed doing some homework. They leave very little because it will soon be the end of the year but they tell us to study, and a lot because the exams will be complicated. I only ran into Thiago twice and everything was fine, and I even thought I had made a new friend but, looking at the matter, I feel that I shouldn't hang out with him, not because he did something he shouldn't do and as I said, I'm not the one to stop judging.

I finished my homework and left the mess on my bed, I just laid down without doing anything else, no noise, no movement, just looking at the ceiling.

I think I'll put something there, a poster or something.

Since I no longer had anything to do, I took my drawing pad and started drawing—once again—the house of my dreams. I have always been interested in what buildings would be like if they were made by me.

Chapter 5

JASMINE

Why does the week go by so fast and slow at the same time? It's Friday and I'm at school, the days go by fast but just when you expect something, time slows down. I found out that the mysterious boy is called Brooke. We became closer and we ate together in the cafeteria. He can't go out but he waits for me every time I go to the store. All good but Mindy is more desperate than usual.

Since I started talking to Brooke, Mindy has tried to talk to him but he's not interested and that makes her act like a *gallina esponjada*. Worst of all, she behaves as if it were my fault, even while talking to herself —Yes, by herself—I heard her say that I tried to take away her "friend". Brooke runs from her, every time the two of us talk and he sees Mindy approaching, he literally runs away.

I'm in my last class and I'm alone, all my classmates have someone to talk to and I don't fit in. I look out the window, the view overlooks the school parking lot and the back of some classrooms. My eyes went to the cars and I couldn't help but see how two people were fighting. I'm not the one to accuse anyone so I just kept watching to see what was happening or if something interesting happened.

But of course, after seeing someone's face, I didn't know what to think, it was Thiago fighting with someone from school. It seemed that they knew each other but they were fighting. If it was me I would be smarter and would go somewhere more private than this. As I supposed, during the week every time I saw him, I avoided talking to him. I wasn't afraid of him but I just didn't want my peace of mind to be interrupted by things I knew I didn't want to know. Okay, maybe I did want to know but I had to remember that curiosity killed the cat.

...but satisfaction brought him back

I kept looking at the two of them as they fought, they pushed each other but what they did the most was yell at each other. After a few minutes they seemed to calm down.

"Miss Santos, is there something much more important outside than paying attention to your class?" The teacher said facing me and everyone stared at me.

"Uhm... no, I..."

"That's what I thought, take out your book, that I will leave homework." Everyone complained, this teacher loves homework and even more if it makes us miserable.

Finally they rang the exit bell and everyone left as if they had the devil inside, I took my time to arrange my things and leave calmly. I looked at the window for the last time, they were no longer there. Once outside the school, I looked at Mindy talking to the school cheerleaders, it was obvious from miles away that they wanted to leave but Mindy held them back.

Those girls are good people and they tend to be nice to everyone and that's a disadvantage if it's Mindy, it would be very rude of them if they go away from her and leave her talking to herself. I continued on my way, I'll go through the mall first, my mom left me since I don't have classes tomorrow.

The way there is a bit bumpy, there are too many people with small businesses, like a market. I stopped at a small stall where they sold old books. They looked neglected but they were by good authors like Charles Dickens and Federico García Lorca. I continued on my way and entered the stores.

I felt someone grab me by the shoulder and I turned immediately with my fist up. But it's Brooke.

"Chill woman."

"*Callate*, what are you doing here?"

"Well, I saw that you were coming here and I wanted to accompany you but I couldn't reach you because there were too many people to go through them."

"Well, whatever, I was going to the clothing stores so I don't think that would interest you." He laughs a little.

"No, they don't but I can entertain myself in another place while you finish your shopping." I smiled at him and then I continued my way.

I had to look for something for tomorrow, my dad will make *carne asada* and my clothes aren't suitable, well it's fine but according to my mom they look like "kitchen rags". While I was looking at the pants someone stopped by my side, seeing his shoes gave me an idea of who he was because I had seen them like three times.

"Hello." I turned to see him.

"Hi…" Okay I'm the guilty party here, I was the one who avoided it and that's why I feel uncomfortable but I did have my reasons.

"I know that maybe you don't want to see me but I really want to be friends, I liked you from the beginning."

"We only looked at each other twice…" I said in a whisper.

I should try to establish a good relationship with him, after all, he has enough problems at home—living with that lady as a mother and a father who only spends his time drinking must be difficult—I looked at Brooke who was coming towards here, I made a sign to him with my hand, he saw me but his expression changed when he saw my company.

"Everything alright, Jas?" He stood next to me and looked at Thiago with disgust.

Not very convinced I said, "Yes, all good." The way he looks at Thiago makes me think he knows him.

Thiago said goodbye and left, Brooke immediately took me out of the store and we walked a bit away from there.

"Do you know him? Do you know Thiago?" So yes, he knows him..

"We've only met a few times and talked but that's all, do you know each other?" He tried to say something but he stopped, he didn't say a word, he just remained thoughtful.

"Yes, but that has nothing to do with it, don't talk to him, it will only cause you problems." I don't know if he knows that this will only make me more curious. "You do know that he was released from prison, right?"

"And how do you know that? You don't have much that you're in town, it doesn't make sense for you to know him and warn me about something you're not supposed to know, not yet at least."

"Just... just don't hang out with him anymore, please! You are my friend and I care about you."

Why do I feel like this won't lead to anything good?

Chapter 6

JASMINE

I'm at home studying, it's Saturday and I have nothing better to do and it would give me the perfect excuse for my mom not to put me to do things. Also, on Monday I have one last exam, it is important that I pass it. But I get bored, I love to read and I could read a book of more than 500 pages but not school stuff, that would kill me, I didn't get even half of the first page.

Brooke hasn't called or texted me, the last time I saw him was yesterday at the mall, and since then I haven't heard from him.

"Jasmine, go to the store!" I hear my mom scream from the kitchen, I know she's there, she's always there.

"*Ya voy!*" I got out of bed and put on some shoes.

I leave the room and go with my mom, she gives me money and a piece of paper, I look at it and see that it is a grocery list. I let out a sigh but still got out. Since it's my last year at school, I should be thinking about what to do with my life, I still don't know what I want to do. As I walk my phone starts to ring, it's a call, without seeing who it was I answered.

"Hello?"

"Jasss, it's me Mindy." And it has to be.

"Hi, what's up?"

"I wanted to know if you wanted to come to my party, I'll have one tonight." A party? I'm actually surprised she's inviting me.

"Sure, I'll see if I can go." I said. I was a little confused but going to a party wouldn't be bad, the only bad thing is that she is the one who is inviting me.

"Excellent! I'll see you later, bye." I couldn't say goodbye back because she hung up immediately.

We finished preparing things for lunch and we just have to wait for the family and friends to arrive. I know the party is today but the truth is I don't feel like going, I feel like there will be a lot of people I don't know. I went to my room to change just like Vanessa. While I was combing my hair I could hear the laughter of some ladies and I swear I recognized who it was.

"*Niñas*, come to say hi!" Yep, I already imagined it. I left and went to the living room, and there was Aunt Suzy.

"But how did they get so big?" Vanessa and I looked at each other. "How are you doing with school?"

That particular aunt is one of those you hope you never see, she meddles in everything and always criticizes everyone's life, oh but if you say something about her it's mean. She thinks that she is right in everything and that her family is super perfect, there are no mistakes and even her dog is the best of all.

My condolences to the dog.

"*Todo bien tia.*" I really don't want to talk to her.

This is how the evening passed, I greeted some cousins and other relatives, I was getting bored. Even my sister had that favorite cousin but I didn't, well, not from my dad's family. I'm the youngest here, in college she's popular with nerds and volunteer activities; she can behave like a little girl here in the house and everything but she is quite a lady.

We even know she's dating someone, she says he's cute and all but it's not what she's looking for.

And I can't even confess!

We were all in the garden and it was already past ten at night. I went into the house but there were people there so I went out front and sat down in front of the door and stayed there. It was a bit cold but I didn't care, it felt good. It's already night but this is going to last until late, my phone vibrates, it was a message.

'Hi Jasy, I wanted to apologize for how I behaved the other day.' It was a message from Brooke.

'Hi, don't worry, we're fine.'

'Are you sure? I don't want you to be mad at me.'

'I'm not.'

I put the phone away and kept looking at the street. I had already been there for more than 20 minutes and I don't know if I should go back inside or stay longer, this neighborhood has always been quiet and there have rarely been any disturbances. I remember once a couple was arrested right in front of the house because they were fighting, why? The man cheated on her with her sister. It was funny to watch because the woman was trying so hard to hit him.

A silhouette began to form along the street, it was tall, I think it was a man. He stood up in the lamplight and I knew who he was, being out this late walking the streets is a little scary coming from him. I waved to him and he waved back. He came closer until he was in front of me.

"Do you mind if I sit next to you?" He says, already standing in front of me.

"Go ahead." He smiled at me and sat down.

"What are you doing out here?" He said and I remember the first time we met.

I smiled and said to him, "I would ask you the same question." I said looking at him.

"Well, it's better to be outside than at home, from what you saw the other day, I don't get along with my folks." So yes, he realized that I saw them.

"I understand. There's a party inside but I didn't want to be there, there's too much hypocrisy and fake faces."

"I see."

None spoke after the small conversation, we just stayed admiring the sky, right now it's very starry. I took the liberty of seeing him in more detail. He has brown skin like cinnamon, long black hair, long eyelashes and I could see the color of his eyes, the color of honey but darker. I looked down a bit and saw that he was wearing a long-sleeved shirt that stuck a little to his arms. I could tell that he was exercising, he is a man with a good body if you ask me.

"So tell me, do you want a photo?" He says to then look at me.
God! He saw that I was staring at him.

"Sorry..."

"Don't worry." He laughs a little and looks straight ahead.

Now that I think about it, his house is on the right and he was coming from the front. I wanted to ask him what he was doing outside at this hour but I didn't say anything, it's not something I should care about. Then I remembered the little argument I had with Brooke.

With a little hesitation I asked, "Can I ask you something?"

"Yeah."

"You and Brooke, do you know each other?" I noticed that he tensed his jaw and scratched his head. I'm not stupid and I know that's like an affirmation. "I guess that's a yes."

"Did he mention something about me or...?"

"Not exactly," he nods.

"I'm just trying to get along with you, I want us to be friends, to be close and I don't want Brooke to be the reason you stop talking to me."

"Why suddenly? We've only met a couple of times."

"That's not true."

Chapter 7

JASMINE

"What do you mean?" I'm confused, we've only talked those two times in the store and once at the mall, and that's all.

"Jasmine, I..." He stopped suddenly when he heard someone running, I also wanted to know who it was, it was late to be running.

Coming from the same direction he came from, a big silhouette approached the light showing that he was a man, a big one and somewhat old. Thiago looked at him and let out a tired sigh, perhaps annoyed. He got up from where he was and looked at me.

"I promise to explain, okay, just let me fix a few things first before we talk." I tried to smile but a grimace came out, and then he left.

He is definitely hiding something. I decided that it was time to go in, when I entered I looked at the group of big cousins talking about whatever they had done. I didn't want to stay so I went to my room, I lay on my bed, I wasn't sleepy and didn't know what to do .

That's how boring I am, I don't even have friends to talk to at this hour.

I knew it was already late, it was about to be one in the morning, besides, I didn't want to text Brooke. He may already be asleep.

THIAGO

I left Jasmine alone and went to talk to one of my contacts, even though it was very risky of me for him to show up when I was still talking to her. I have to explain a few things to her before stupid Brooke tells her the wrong things. We came to a park not far from my street.

I wanted to get this over with quickly so I asked, "What do you have for me?"

"As expected, the family wants to feed you to the dogs, they want you dead and say you shouldn't have messed with them." He laughs a little but I don't, what I did was wrong but I don't regret having done it.

"What about the other man?"

"His relatives?" I nod, "His wife knows that he is no longer in this world but his daughters still don't know, can I know what he did?"

"The same as the other."

"I see, you take 'don't look, don't talk and don't listen' very seriously when it comes to her." I don't look at him, I just keep thinking that surely what I do will not lead me to good, but I would do anything as long as she doesn't have to worry about anything.

"Go away, I'll call you when I need you." He didn't say anything and he was about to leave but he stopped and handed me his hand. I know what he wants. "I don't have cash at the moment but I'll write you a check."

I took out my wallet and from there a check that was already written. I gave it to him and he left.

I spent these two years thinking about her, thinking about how she's been, wondering if she's been sure, if she's changed, and I can for sure say that she only got more beautiful. I take one last look around and head back the way I came. I got to her house and stared at the window of her room. The lights are not on but there is a dim light, I suppose it's on her phone or there is a lamp on.

I continue on my way, I arrive at my house and being at the entrance I receive a notification on my phone.

Brooke.

'You should leave her alone, you wouldn't like her to know what you're doing'

That bastard.

I don't reply to him and I don't get another message either, I don't understand how those two came to be friends but I can't let Jasmine find out about the things I've done, it was all because of her but I know she wouldn't understand, she doesn't have the twisted mind like me. I entered my house and went up to my room, when I killed the other in my room I forgot to close the windows and I noticed that she was there with her mother. I can't say for sure that she didn't see anything but I hope not.

I still remember when I looked at her for the first time, the time I decided that she would be mine, only mine and nobody else's, I didn't care what I had to do or the time it would take me but I only knew one thing and that is that Jasmine Santos is untouchable for everyells, except me.

Since I was little I knew that something was wrong with me, I fought a lot and my temper hung by a thread. When I was 10 years old, I hit a boy in my class so much that they had to send him to the hospital because I had broken his nose. The reason was because he had grabbed my things and nobody touched my things. As I grew up, everything got worse since my parents did not have enough money for my treatment and they were—and are—irresponsible. I would be incapable of harming Jasmine but whoever dares to harm her in any way... I'll make sure they never do it again.

The next day, I woke up in a good mood. I knew I had a chance to see Jasmine at the store, so I washed up and changed before going downstairs and leaving. When leaving the house, I immediately noticed that today it would be hot, too hot.

I hope she's wearing something cool... wait...

I hurried to go to the store and, definitely, there she was. I recognized some of her cousins, they were buying a lot of drinks and some flavored ice. I looked at Jasmine, she was wearing shorts and a sleeveless top.

Damn it! She looks hot.

"*Jasmine, apurate! Aqui hace calor.*"

"*Ya voy.*" She says as she takes some juices from the fridge.

I entered the store and the dispatcher greeted me, Jasmine turned and looked at me, she gave me a small wave with her hand and her cousins noticed it. Several of them were giving her little pushes and that seemed to bother her, and as I had said before, I didn't care what I did as long as she didn't have bad feelings about anything.

With the most annoying expression I told them, "All of you are getting in the way, would you do me a big favor and move?" They gave me the expression I expected and that gave me satisfaction.

They moved from the door and I opened it so I could get my drink. I looked at her and without the others seeing me, I winked at her. I got out of there and went to pay. Leaving the store I went to the shade of a tree. I knew that they didn't find it pretty but that's what happens if they bother her I hope she would have found it funny.

I decided to wait until they left the store, so I could see her one more time.

Chapter 8

JASMINE

I didn't expect Thiago to do something like that, and I must admit that it made me laugh to see the naive faces of my cousins. We pay for our purchase and leave the store.

I saw that he was leaning against a tree that was across the street, he was looking in my direction, I gave him a smile and continued on my way. We got home and the first thing one of my cousins did was tell one of my aunts what happened.

My aunt asks worriedly, "Was he rude to you?"

"Yes." I knew that it didn't affect them in the slightest but in order to attract attention they are happy to exaggerate things.

But yeah, he was rude to them. But I don't understand why he did it.

"Besides, I think he knows Jasmine, they said 'hi' as if they were friends." My mom heard that and approached us.

"What boy are you talking about?" She says while putting a hand on her waist.

"He is tall, has brown skin and black hair, he looks older." My mom immediately saw me.

"Jasmine, it better not be that boy, because if it is, *ni te la acabas,* you know very well that I want you away from that house and its people." Says my mom scolding me and they all stare at me.

"*Si ma...*"

Out of shame I went to my room, I shouldn't start my day like this. I closed the door and sat in the small armchair that I had there. It is not the first time that my mom has put me through this situation in front of the family. It's barely one in the afternoon and I don't know what to do. On Sundays I usually go to the mall but I don't want to go with anyone. I'll try to ask if I can go alone.

I went out and looked for my mom, several relatives stayed to sleep and there were too many people in this small house. I found her talking to Vanessa.

"Mom, can I go to the mall?"

"Go but take one of your cousins, ask them if they want to go."

"Can I go alone? *Porfi.*" I said quietly.

"Ask them or else you won't go." There goes my desire to go.

"*Ma*, let her go, after all nothing will happen to her." My mom looked at her and was left in doubt, "And I don't think she'll go alone, her friend will go, *esa niña*, Mindy." Vanessa knew how I felt about Mindy but my mom loved that girl.

"Okay go, *pero te me cuidas.*" I almost jumped with excitement.

Being ready, I left the house in a hurry so that no cousin would ask me and want to come with me. It was a long way to walk to the mall so I decided to take the bus. While I was waiting, I received a message.

'Jas, what are you doing?' It's Brooke.
'I'm on my way to the mall.'
'Super, see you there.'

The strangest conversation I've ever had.

I arrived at my destination and I didn't know whether to really wait for Brooke or just walk, I decided on the second option. While I walked

I looked at the people, I looked at how each one of them had the way they dressed, the way they acted and their way of walking through the crowd; after all, this is Los Angeles. In this big city the expression of each one became easy to liberate—some crazier than others—but there are also too many cultures that do not allow to be received with that "freedom".

At home, for example, I can't go get a tattoo because I know my mom would say something like "are you into drugs?" "Are you in a gang?" "How ridiculous!", she would think the worst of me.

I stopped at a shoe store, went in to see and I noticed that they put some very nice black platform ankle boots for sale. I would like to afford to buy some but I am not working at the moment and the little money I have I use it for my needs.

Another day Jasmine...

I kept looking in the store, there were several people looking, I stopped to see how a couple was trying on matching shoes, it would be nice to do that but not so obvious, that would be too much for me. I would like to have matching jewelry, such as bracelets, earrings,... rings.

After walking a few more minutes I stopped at a milkshake stand. I made my order and waited, I hadn't looked at Brooke the whole time I've been here, I guess he just said it to play.

"Order for Jasmine?" I heard my name said and I got up to take my order, I thanked and sat down again.

"And my milkshake?" Says someone who stopped in front of me, I looked up to see him.

"I really thought you wouldn't come."

"I said I was coming. Since I'm here, I'll ask for one myself." I nodded and went back to my business with my milkshake.

I ordered a chocolate milkshake with enough milk to make it not so thick, strawberry caramel, and whipped cream with dried strawberries on top. A delight. Brooke sat in the chair opposite, in addition to his milkshake, he also had a glazed donut.

"*Provecho.*" I told him and he looked at me with confusion. "It is something that is said to people who are about to eat, like the French when they say '*Bon appetit*' when giving you food, it doesn't have an exact word in English."

"Okay…"

We drank our milkshakes while we talked about random things, he told me a little more about his family; Brooke is an only child, his father is American and his mother Canadian, they started living here after they got married. We stopped talking for a moment, it was a comfortable silence, just enjoying our company. I took that silence to observe him. Brooke is fair skinned, light brown hair, blue eyes, a few freckles and he's tall, I know he's into that sport where he runs and jumps so he's skinny but fit.

I finished my milkshake and I was going to tell him that I had to go but I remembered that there was still an unresolved issue.

"I'll ask you a question and I really want you to answer me truthfully." He looked at me and nodded, so I continued, "What do you and Thiago have in between?

He was silent and he got serious, he was just looking at me. What am I doing? This is not something I should meddle in, I've barely been knowing Brooke for about two weeks and I've known Thiago for days, I'm not the best friend of any of them or a close friend of them. I guess this is one of the reasons why I don't have too many friends, I meddle where I shouldn't.

I immediately apologized, "Sorry, I'm not the one to ask you to tell me things you don't want." I felt stupid, if I continue like this I'll lose him.

"Jasmine…"

I interrupted him before he said anything else. "Leave it like that," I said with a forced smile. "See you at school, bye." I got up and almost ran from the place.

I left the mall and started to feel bad. I think it's a defect of mine to 'attack' people in their personal matters. I have to stop doing that.

Now that I think about it, since I was a child I have always wanted to know things about those around me, not because I was nosy, it's because I was interested in the person, I was interested in knowing about them.

Chapter 9

JASMINE

I was coming to my street but first I went through the park, I saw a bench and I sat down.

It was definitely not a good idea to have insisted on the subject, Brooke and Thiago became uncomfortable asking about their relationship, I suppose they have a history and not a very pretty one. Brooke says that I shouldn't go near Thiago, Thiago only gets a little upset if I ask about Brooke.

Unless…

I raised my head when I had that crazy thought, I don't want to think about it but if it would, it actually makes sense, at first glance I would say that they are not "like that".

Maybe that's why they can't stand each other, not even for the thought.

Thiago worried that Brooke had told me something, something that has to do with him. I have no other way of thinking about the matter. It all leads me to the same thing. I'll make sure to apologize to both of them, it's none of my business, it's a matter of two.

I got out of the shower and went into my room, changed into my pajamas, brushed my hair and went to bed. On Monday there are too many things to do, arriving at school. In my first class, I have a history exam and after that another, English, for the end of classes I have to stay to help a teacher move from room, why me? I'm the most "friendly" of her class, according to her.

I don't even pay attention to her class.

That's how I fell asleep, with those and more thoughts about everything. Overthinking things tires me but it's something I can't help.

My alarm goes off and I get up, I start my morning routine; I finish getting ready and go out.

My parents saw me and said, "Good morning." I walked over and kissed them on the cheek.

"Good morning, I'll go first, I have many things to do and I want to give an advance." I tell them while I grab an orange.

When I open the door my mom tells me, "Okay, be careful." And then I left.

I leave the house and this time I go faster. I go house after house, some neighbors go out for a walk with the dog, others stretch to start their morning walk and so on, everyone doing their routines. I pass by Thiago's house and I see that he is coming out of it, he is dressed in sportswear, he is going to run I suppose.

"Good morning." He greets me, waving his hand.

"Morning. Hey, you think we can see each other after school?" When I tell him that he smiles out of nowhere.

"Yes of course!"

I continued on my way and arrived at the school, I saw Brooke get out of a car and I took the opportunity to approach him and talk.

"Good morning." I said as I was next to him.

"Hi Jasy, how is your morning going?"

"It's okay, thanks, I wanted to ask you if we can meet after school?"

"Yep, see you I'm in a hurry or else the math teacher will send me to detention." He says and runs off.

Well at least I can apologize to both.

I entered the school and went straight to my classroom, I still have a few minutes to study before classes start and with it the exam.

And that's how my morning and part of the afternoon went. During my break, my lunch hour, I called a restaurant for food and went out to wait for my order. While I was waiting I noticed how someone was approaching me quickly, and the closer she got I noticed who it was.

She bluntly says, "We need to talk."

"Hi to you too, Mindy."

"What are you up to with Brooke?" There she goes again, "I try to talk to him but he doesn't even deign to see me, I ask him to explain something to me and he says he doesn't understand but someone else asks him and out of nowhere he's the smartest."

Confused, I ask, "and why do you think I have something to do with it?"

"I know you're doing something, what did you tell him? To not come near me? Did you tell him that I'm a bad person?" She is acting like a crazy person, they didn't give her 'drugs'.

"*Tu tas' loca.*"

"What did you say?" Lucky me that she doesn't know Spanish.

"Nothing, I just haven't done anything."

"You better, because Jasmine," she comes closer until she is face to face with me. "You wouldn't want to know what it feels like to be truly isolated." She says before leaving the way she came.

What the heck was that? Did Mindy just threaten me?

The delivery man brought me my food and I paid him. I looked at the time, in two minutes I'm going back to class. I'm not ordering food again.

I entered school and went to my next class, I'll have time to eat; my next class is Spanish and I really hate that class and the teacher, why? Well, it happens that the Spanish they use to "teach us" is Castilian

Spanish and the teacher really thinks that this type of Spanish is the same that the entire Hispanic community speaks.

You are so wrong mi amigo!

Classes are over and now I'm going to the back of the school, where I would see the boys. I got to where a bench was and sat down to wait for them, minutes later I saw Brooke approaching.

"Hi," he hugs me and I give him a smile as we separate. "So, what did you want to talk about?"

"Thiago is still missing." When mentioning his name, his smile faded.

"Did you also call him? Jasmine, why did you do that?" When I was going to tell him, I saw that Thiago was already coming, and as I supposed, his smile also faded when he saw that Brooke was here too.

"What is this?" He said when he arrived.

Well, here I go, "Guys, don't get angry, I wanted to talk to both of you and above all apologize, and the best way was to get y'all together without you knowing."

Thiago asks confused, "apologize for what? You didn't do anything wrong."

"It's just that after the little conversations we had and I was asking questions, I noticed that you both got upset or uncomfortable when I mentioned the other's name," they listened carefully. "And I came to understand that you have stuff to deal with and I understand it."

"Really?" Brooke says surprised.

"Yes, I don't know why it surprises you, I'm not the type of person who judges."

With a face of disbelief he asked, "Do you really not care what he has done?"

"Brooke, I know that maybe he did something to you and hurt you and that's why you don't like being with him but it's not something that should matter to me, that's why I wanted to apologize."

"Jasmine, I think you have the wrong idea." Thiago says as he approaches next to us.

"It's fine, I really don't care about people's preferences, I have a cousin who also likes boys and I understand how difficult it can be to express it and if you haven't done it, it's great!"

They both go blank for a moment and then seem to react.

...

...

...

"WHAT?!"

Chapter 10

BROOKE

Really, I am surprised that she came to such a crazy conclusion, that piece of shit and me as a couple? Not even in her craziest dreams would something like this happen, and if I were gay, he wouldn't even be the fifth option.

"Jasy, I think you're wrong."

"I have to go, I agreed to help a teacher, see you!" She says and runs away.

"Well, I didn't expect that." Thiago says as he watches her leave and I stand in front of him. "Now what do you want?"

"You know what I want."

"Well, it won't happen, I'm not going to leave her just because you ask me to and in any case I'm going to explain a little about the real problem and not this nonsense."

I said sarcastically, "Oh, really?" I stood in front of him and as if it were the most normal thing in the world I said to him, "What are you going to tell her? 'Jasmine, Imma murderer with mental problems and I can't control my anger?' Are you going to tell Jasmine that?

"Not like that…"

"Then how? I really don't want you to corrupt her mind, she's at peace and her only problem is that unbearable girl but it's normal school stuff, she doesn't need a stalker."

"I'm not a stalker! And apparently you are the one obsessed with her, tell me, do you like Jasmine?" I notice how he tenses when pronouncing that question.

"Yes, I do but not like in the way you think, she's my friend, I see her as a sister, my little sister, and that's why I'll protect her from guys like you, do you think I didn't find out that you sent someone to invade her room?"

He tensed when he heard me. "How do you know that?"

"Do you think I wouldn't find out? Thiago, for a reason we know each other. I will not repeat it again, stay away from her, and another thing, don't speak to her family because it will be worse for her."

I decided to leave here, I didn't mind leaving him alone and I continued on my way.

I know where Jasmine is, I would go and explain to her what she thinks is wrong but better another time; before I went home, I went to a convenience store, I had to refill my refrigerator.

The dispatcher sees me and greets me, "Hi boy, how are ya'?"

"I'm okay, how's your wife?"

"She's fine, thanks for asking."

"No problem."

I kept looking through the shelves and I stopped at the liquor section. I was tempted to buy one but I don't want to give the man any trouble, I still have two years to go before I can buy alcohol... legally. Well less than two years now. I take other things and I'm going to pay. When I finish I grab my bags and get in my car.

I'm in the living room watching TV but I can't pay attention to it, the only thing on my mind is how the hell does that bastard know Jasmine,

I've been knowing Thiago for years and at no time did it seem to me that he cared about anyone else, he It's not like that, he only cares about himself.

I get up from the sofa and go up to my room, when I enter I sit at my desk and start to do my thing.

I still remember in detail the day Thiago reach to me for help, he wanted me to help him enter a house that had a security system, it was not something difficult to do but I always wondered why he entered that house, he only entered and came out after a few minutes, he had nothing in his hands. Just a paper. We didn't meet in person until a year later.

From that night he kept looking for me for things like that or to enter cell phones, he paid me good money to do it so I accepted every task. Only once, I refused to make one of his requests, Thiago wanted me to get him weapons, he wanted me to ask for them without being detected because I was still a kid, I was afraid that the police would come for me, of course everything else I could still get in trouble but it was something simple and this was out of my level. After that, three days later, I found out that the police were after him. That was two years ago!

So yeah, how the hell does he know Jasmine?

I typed codes every time I broke down a barrier in the system so nothing could detect me, I entered the computer's camera and, bingo! Now I can see her. Now yes, I can know what that crazy woman is up to.

Mindy was using her computer, I could see what she was doing on my other monitor. She was sending messages with endless people, several of them are from the school but also others from other schools. From what little I could see of her room, it seemed to be a normal room, it's pink, white furniture and I think it had a window.

I looked at her messages and it really worried me, she treated more than five of them as if they were a couple or something more than just friends, but it was sick because apparently they were older men.

"Come on baby, send me a picture of how I like it."
"Mindy, be a good girl and touch yourself for me."
"If you want us to stay together, you will have to submit to me."
"Look how you put me." *photo*

I stopped reading, this was making me nauseous. Mindy is 18 years old and if she wants her life to be like that, then so be it, but I really want her to leave Jasmine alone and me, of course.

Rubbing my face I said, "This girl is crazy." I looked at the time. "It's late…"

I didn't have much to do, it's late but it's not night, I'm home alone and I don't know what to do. I can't go and bother my parents because I don't live with them. I regret not insisting that I wanted a brother when I was a child. I leave my room and go to the kitchen, I'll see if I can cook something.

I'm going to cook because I'm bored? Yep.

I entered the kitchen and was going to grab a frying pan but I saw that the fruit bowl was on the left side of the island, I always put it on the right side. I turned and scanned around. I have a condition called OCD, it's not serious, and I don't usually change the way I put my things. If something is out of place I'll notice it, I don't care if it is just an inch or a centimeter.

I looked around my kitchen and noticed that there was a poorly closed cabinet. I know that this is his thing, no one other than my family knows where I live and I know that Thiago manages to know things about other people, including me.

I approached to see what it was, there was only a note that had a hand drawn with the middle finger standing.

"How childish you are."

Chapter 11

JASMINE

It's been two weeks since I talked to both boys. In that time the school gave us all kinds of homework, exams, extraocular activities and more, all so that we have "good preparation" for entering a good university. The good news is that after today we have a week off.

My sister finally made up her mind and officially started dating that guy she's been talking to. Now he comes home often and apparently my dad likes the boy.

What happened to Mindy? Well, I tried to avoid her at all costs, since that day when she threatened me I stopped speaking to her, it was obvious that I was not going to do what she asked me to do but seriously she proposed to spy on me, I even get chills when I go to the bathroom! I didn't tell anyone about it, I didn't feel like it was something really dangerous.

I arrived at my history room. The teacher was an old man, he is a good person and I like how he teaches his class. The only bad thing he has is that when we give him the work he gave us, the work has to be perfect.

I hear someone shout, "Jasy!" I look up to see who it is. "You have no idea how much I've missed you, we barely even talked."

Imitating the same energy as Brooke, I responded, "I would say the same but my homework stole all my attention."

"I understand you, I still haven't finished a project from my physics class. Before I forget it! I really need you to know that what you thought about the idiot and me is not true, it's nothing like that."

"What? About being a couple?"

"Yes! Thiago and I are not that, I'm not even gay or bi."

Trying to understand, I ask, "So you're not a couple or exes?"

"Exactly! We are nothing like that."

"So why do you two act like that?" Deep down, I thought it had to do with whatever Thiago did or does but I didn't want to, Brooke is someone very sweet to be involved in that world.

"I really would like to tell you but I'm afraid of how you would react." Before I could say anything the teacher came in giving instructions, Brooke went to his seat and I just kept thinking about what he said.

What did they do?

Classes finally ended, it was time to rest from school. I left school and was going to go straight home but I looked at Brooke and remembered what he said. I really would like to know his relationship with Thiago but I'm not someone trustworthy, for a reason he doesn't tell me. But what do I think! He doesn't owe me any explanation, no reason, it's their thing.

But I want to know!

I decided to continue on my way, the day was cloudy, I guess it's going to rain.

I got to see Thiago's house, I remember that the first time I saw it was when I thought I saw a person being strangled. What nonsense. As I passed it I looked at a woman sitting in that rocking chair.

We glanced at each other and I smiled out of courtesy, she didn't return my smile and took a cigarette to her mouth.

I have to remember that not everyone has manners in this place.

If I remember correctly I think she is Thiago's mother, she looks very young. Now that I think about it, how old is Thiago? He doesn't go to school, he will be over 19 then. I got home, went in and immediately looked at a note in the vase on the coffee table.

It's a note from my parents.

"Hija, fuimos a un mandado tu papá y yo, Vanessa no estará en la casa, fue a una salida con su novio. Hay comida en el refri."

So home alone?

I went to my room and left my stuff on the bed. I really didn't have anything to do, I don't have homework and I don't feel like doing anything productive. I decide to read something, I take one of my favorite books and start reading.

Even the protagonist has more fun things to do, or something more interesting to do... Well, at this moment they have kidnapped her but even I know that her man, six feet tall, will arrive and save her.

It seems that just asking someone to bring me a rose or a letter is a lot to ask. I stopped looking at the book for a second to look at the time, an hour had already passed. I feel my phone vibrate, I grab it and see that it is a message from an unknown number.

> 'Hello, Jasmine, I'm Thiago.' How did he get my number?
> 'Really? Prove it.'
> 'The other day you said that Brooke and I had a relationship, which is not true, and you left without me being able to tell you that it is not true, I already said that it is not true?'
> 'Ok, ok,' this only confirms my suspicion more and more.

We talked a bit but then he said goodbye because he had things to do. At least I know how old he is, 21 years old. He is two years older than me. I left my phone on the bed, left and went to the kitchen, I was already hungry. I was startled when I heard lightning.

Yup, it's going to rain.

I opened the fridge and took the plate with food that my mom had left. It's possible that they stayed talking with one of their friends, it's always like that when the two of them go out. They'll be very late then. My sister... I really don't even want to think about what she was doing, I wasn't born yesterday.

I put the food to heat up and I stayed there waiting for it to be ready.

I should get a job, it's not long before I get out of school and I want to have some money before I can look for a university. But lately I have had bad luck. I have applied in many places these days and I have not been accepted anywhere. I don't know how many times I have lied in my job application to make it perfect or at least passable but nothing seems to work. I even gave honest answers.

I'm starting to feel like a failure.

My parents know and they always tell me that everything will come in due time, that soon I will be able to see something good but I demand a lot from myself and for anything that doesn't work out for me I start to feel bad, it doesn't matter if it's not a big deal for others, but for me it is.

I'm already 19 years old and many people my age are already working, they have their own place and I even know that some of them from school have already been accepted into their dream universities.

I can't even work at McDonalds.

Chapter 12

JASMINE

Turkey week is very tiring, my mom just spends her time going to and from the store buying things for dinner, she has Vanessa and I like *chachas* all over the house so we don't have to worry on most days of cleaning, and for us to be able to help her with food.

My dad will be in charge of preparing the turkey and I don't know what other things, the fact is that in this house you don't just do nothing.

"Jasmine, go to the store!" Why is it always me?

"Okay." She gave me money and I left the house.

Well, at least I have a few minutes of rest while I go to the store.

I got to the store and grabbed what I needed, while I was doing it I looked at Mindy with a boy in the candy section. He looked older but it's not something that concerns me. Having already everything I went to a cashier.

I hear a shrill voice behind me. "What a surprise!" No, it is not.

I greeted reluctantly, "Mindy, hi.."

"Look, I present to you a friend." She hugged him by the arm and looked at me waiting for something, a reaction maybe.

Weird that she said "a friend" and not "my friend."

"That's good." I paid for my things and grabbed the bag but I shouldn't have thought that I could leave that easily.

She stopped me from passing to tell me, "Jasmine, I noticed that you don't talk to me like before, I don't want you to think that after what I told you, I didn't want you to be my friend anymore, I would be super happy if we were besties again!" She says with an exaggerated smile.

Really, I didn't believe what I was hearing, that she didn't realize that what she told me was a threat? I would not feel comfortable continuing to be "friends" with her or someone like that. Hardly anyone at school realizes how toxic she is and very few see it.

But that doesn't matter to her, because those who know what she is like are normal students. Students like me who don't stand out in the student community.

I said quickly, "We'll see, bye." And I left the store.

It is Saturday! I know I don't have classes for the rest of the week but a Saturday always means I can relax however I like. I was going to grab my sister's computer and I was going to watch a movie with some popcorn but my phone started ringing, it's a call.

"*Mande?*" I answered without looking at who it was.
"Hi, *boneca*."
"*Boneca*? What word is that?"
"A pretty one."
"Whatever, what do you want?"
"Will you do something today?" I don't want to think that I know where this is going but I think I do know where this is going.
"Nope."
"I want us to go out, can we go to the park or just have a walk?" Go out with him? I can do it but…

I thought about it but I said yes, I hung up and quickly went to tell my mom that I'm going out with a friend, she said yes but be careful and don't be late.

I closed the door of my room and started looking for something to wear. I have nice clothes but I don't know what to wear for this, are we only supposed to walk?

And I'm not supposed to be the type of person that has a lot of clothes and nothing to wear.

I looked through all my clothes and in the end I decided on a gray jean with a bit of blue, a white tank top, a cream-colored knitted sweater,—because it's a bit cold—and black ankle boots. I look in the mirror and feel like I'm not that bad. As I grab a handbag I receive a message.

'I'm outside.'

I leave my room and say goodbye to my mom. I open the door and there it is. He's dressed in black, baggy pants and a long-sleeved collared shirt, he looks good.

"Hey." I greet him with a smile and he smiles at me the same.

"Hi, you look good."

I smiled and thanked him, "Thank you."

As we walked we talked about all sorts of things.

"Really, I swear! My *tia* said that she made a Muslim fall in love with her and when we asked her how she did it she said 'with my good food, I made him a *pozole* and he loved it'." We both started laughing.

"I don't want to be rude but at least most people know that they don't eat pork."

"I know!" We were already in the park and we sat on a bench.

"It seems that you have an entertaining family."

"Something like that, good times are almost always when there is something to celebrate or just because they are drinking, drinking a lot is in the family."

"Do you drink?" I laughed at his question.

"Even if you don't believe it, I'm not that stupid, being here I wouldn't drink a drop, only if I'm in Mexico yes, the age of majority to drink is 18."

"What a luck then." Thiago suddenly became serious. "Before I couldn't clarify things well because I was afraid of how you would react but I feel like I won't know until you know." I think this is the same reason Brooke told me.

"Know what?"

"Brooke doesn't have much to do with this, that's a matter for another time, but the truth is that I…" He turned his head towards me and looked at me. "The reason I was in prison was because I…"

We heard a loud scream from behind us, "THIAGO!"It was Brooke who was almost running towards us. "Don't even think about it!"

We both got up from the bench and I looked at Brooke a little worried. "Brooke, what's going on?"

"Jasy, I know you want to know things but please don't let him tell you, because I know he would lie to you." They both gave each other a hateful look

Now I really don't understand anything, all this will give me a headache, I know I insisted on knowing why they don't get along with each other but I think this is too much drama, whatever Thiago did to get him jailed must have been something very bad, I know people who have done everything, in Mexico everything happens, but I was never friends with those people.

I was getting annoyed, so I told them, "Relax both of you. You know what, why don't we just leave this as it is and we all go back to our normal lives, okay?"

They both ignored me and talked to each other. Thiago gets face to face with Brooke and says, "You should stop meddling where they don't call you, *menino*."

"Do not come to me with your idiocies, this involves me whether you want it or not." Thiago takes him by the shirt and begins to speak in another language, something that took me by surprise

"*Eu vejo o que acontece aqui, você não quer que ela saiba o que você fez.*"

"*Não sabe o que você diz.*"

"*Ah, claro que sei.*"

Chapter 13

JASMINE

Portuguese, they are speaking Portuguese... since when do they know how to speak Portuguese?! They both talk to each other and apparently Thiago said something that bothered Brooke and he almost tried to hit him.

"*YA!*You guys are acting like little kids!" They separate and look at me. "You know what, I better go, you two get along well but leave me out, *adios*."

When I asked for something of interest in my life, I didn't mean this! I don't want to be that person who is in the middle of conflicts, but I think I am that character.

I walked to my house, when I got there I entered and went straight to my room. When he asked me out I didn't think it would end like this. I laugh a little pointlessly. What did I think would happen? That this would be like a date? Yes, of course. I get undressed and put on my pajamas, it's barely five in the afternoon but I don't care, I'm not going out all day anyway.

I lay on my bed and started watching videos on my phone, there wasn't much to see but there were too many videos about decorations and things like that.

"Are you okay?" I turn around and see that Vanessa is leaning against the door frame.

"Yes, why?"

"I noticed you were very down when you got here." She walks over and sits on the edge of the bed. "Did something happen?"

"Not really." I think I was more disappointed by the fact that nothing happened.

"Do you wanna talk about it?"

I was silent for a few seconds but then I spoke, "It's just... you know I don't go out much and I don't have many friends to do it with. Today a friend invited me out, we just walked and talked but it felt nice, you know." She listens to me carefully, "I think I expect too much, we hardly know each other but he is a good boy."

She says, a little surprised, "Oh, so it's a 'he'?" I laughed a little."

Okay, lie, he's not a good boy, "good boys" don't go to prison.

"Yes, but something happened and nothing turned out as I thought it would, I really just wanted to have a good start, you know, like they show in the movies or in the books."

"Yes, I understand what you say."

"I don't think you do, you are a nerd and you are popular at that, very friendly and sociable and you have a boyfriend."

"I don't know whether to feel flattered or offended about the nerd thing." We both laughed. "But let me tell you something, I made an effort to have those grades and to be able to be sociable whether I wanted to or not, I had to talk to people, when I had doubts I had to ask teachers or my classmates."

"I try too but nothing seems to happen."

"*Todo a su tiempo*, like grandpa says '*Con el tiempo y paciencia se adquiere la ciencia*'."

We talked for a while but after she had to leave, she had two classes to go to. She goes to the university and apparently she is doing well, besides she only goes two or three times a week.

Another little while later I looked at my watch, it was already late and I didn't feel like staying up all night so I better fell asleep.

BROOKE

"I really congratulate you, do you think I was going to let you brainwash her?"

"You are so wrong, I don't know what bull-shit you think but let me tell you something, I would be unable to hurt her."

"You don't even know that! Did you see how she was when she left? She had an annoyed expression, and do you know whose fault it was? Well, yours."

"Don't come at me with that, it was your fault, we were both very well before you arrived." We were both upset and I don't really care that people are staring at us.

"I already told you, I don't want you near her, I know that today you managed so that I didn't know that you were here, but let me remind you that I am much smarter than you."

"*Pedaço de merda.*"

"You are the piece of shit!"

I no longer wanted to be with that idiot anymore, I left there and went home. When I arrived, the first thing I did was get on my computer, the fact that Thiago knows what I did only makes things more difficult, that I "threatened" him that I would tell Jasy about his things was only to scare him off, It wouldn't be so nice of me to put her in that situation, I wouldn't be the good friend.

Thiago should take care of his big mouth, I won't be so nice next time.

At midnight, I decided to go out and go to the cemetery. I know that no one normally would do it at this time but for that same reason I will go. I arrived and entered, looking for the name of the person I wanted to visit, until I found it.

"I'm back, I know maybe you didn't want to see me but I did." I adjust my jacket because it's getting colder, I continued talking, "I didn't come to apologize if that's what you expect, I just wanted to see that you were still there, buried. I met a girl, she's pretty and kind but I see her as a sister to me but your stupid cousin wants her for himself, I know you don't care about all this I'm telling you but I would really appreciate it if you bewitched him tonight, I know you hate him too, after all, we both put you where you are."

I said goodbye and left that place. I know there were things I didn't want to do but putting that bastard to sleep was for the good of both of us.

He sometimes came with Thiago to see me to do one of his jobs, he wasn't very smart and that was a risk. One time the three of us went to do a job and they almost discovered us because that bastard only wanted to make a mess.

Thiago and I talked and we decided that it was not a good idea for his cousin to continue living. He realized on the first attempt and threatened to go to the police and give us away, on the second attempt we almost succeeded but this time he was smarter and he almost killed us.

The motherfucker was smart when he wanted to.

On the third attempt, it was me who ended his life, well almost, Thiago gave him the final blow. It was something that we both decided never to mention, but what he doesn't know is that I left a memory in the idiot's clothes, in that memory was all the evidence of what we've both done, why did I do it? Last resort I guess.

If someone, for whatever reason, dug up that idiot's body, they would find all the work we've done. Well, as far as he was still alive, of course.

I got home and checked that Thiago hadn't done anything, again, then I just went to sleep.

Chapter 14

JASMINE

It is already November 20 and that means that the family that comes from far away will come, the good thing is that it is the family that I like. It's on my mom's side.

"*Niña*, come and help me get the blankets and mattresses out of the closet"

"Coming."

We took everything out of the closet and put them in a corner of the living room. Some cousins would stay in my room—and me, of course—but my uncles and aunts in the living room, we have too many relatives and this house isn't very big. I helped my mom put away other things, just like my sister, and then we stopped to eat. My dad is working and will rest for the next four days.

While I was washing the dishes, my mom and Vanessa were talking.

"*Ma'*, today is Monday, remember that we must take out the garbage."

"*Ay, si cierto.*"

The family arrived and the four of us are receiving them, greetings and hugs for not having seen them since I don't know when. Most of my cousins were boys and only three or four girls.

My cousin, the one I love the most, jumps on me and we hug, "Jasmine! Long time without seeing you."

"I know!" I hugged my cousin but as I had said before, there is always that family member that you don't like.

"*Pa'*, I didn't want to come." Says one of my cousins to her dad.

"Take off that *tacuache* face and go say hello to your *tios*." And with a bad face she greeted my parents and us.

Leaving all that awkward moment aside, we all started to do something at home, the women started to see what they would cook that very day and the men wanted to make *carne asada*, why? For the simple fact that the family came, instead the cousins began to talk about what had happened to us—them—all this time that we did not see each other.

A cousin told us about her love life, "Well I ended up with the boyfriend I had, the fucking *vato* only looked at the others' asses!"

My sister, with a disbelieving face said, "Karla but that is already the fifth."

"AND? *Vida solo hay una.*"

"That is only said when you will do something or very stupid or just to make an excuse for what you are going to do." We all laughed.

"I know I'm not the only one who has done stupid things, besides, having a boyfriend is not stupid."

"No, but when you change boyfriends like when you change *calzones* yes it is."

Karla, to get rid of the attention, talks to me, "And what about you, Jasmine?"

"*Yo?* Well... not much, nothing really." I said, a little uncomfortable, the truth is that I prefer to listen to them.

"Really? Not a boyfriend? Drama? A murder?" He says the last thing as a joke but the first thing that came to mind was Thiago.

Why am I thinking about him?

I thought a little before answering but not much came to mind. "Nope, well the only drama I have is that there is a girl in my class who gives me a headache with her presence."

"Really? Why?"

"I think I had told you about her, her name is Mindy, do you remember her?" I still told them a little about how things are, I didn't go into details.

"Ah, yes, I think that she came to the house when we were visiting. I remember that she tried to flirt with me but she is *muy encimosa*."

"She flirts with everyone as long as they give her attention and the more "important" you are, the better."

"But he's not important." We all laughed at what Karla said and continued talking.

It got dark and the adults went to sleep, we stayed awake, we talked about other things, we played a little, my mom scolded us because we were too noisy, we watched movies and in the end we fell asleep around four in the morning .

I woke up to a small noise that went on and on and didn't stop. I looked for what it was and I saw that it's my phone vibrating, I looked at who it was, it's Brooke.

What does he do at this time?

"Hello..." my voice was a little hoarse.
"I woke you up?"
No! Why do you think that? Baboso.
"Yes, what's up?"
"Sorry, I wanted to know how you were."
"Couldn't you wait until tomorrow?" There was silence and I almost went back to sleep.
"Jasmine?"
"What?"
"Do you think we can meet tomorrow to talk?" I don't

really want to, like for what happened the other day to happen again, *pues no.*

I looked around, "I don't know…" My cousins were still sleeping, it's good that I didn't wake them up.

"I understand if you don't want to, I know that the last time we saw each other was not pleasant at all."

"Yup."

"Then I let you sleep, sorry for waking you up."

"Okay, bye."

"Bye." We both hung up and I fell asleep immediately.

I woke up and saw that I was the second, my cousin was already awake but on his phone, I said good morning and did the same as him. I had notifications from my social networks but also a message, I thought it would be from Brooke but it's from Thiago.

'I know we are probably giving you a headache and I want to apologize, all this should not have been like this.'

What happened that made them want to apologize on the same day? And time apparently.

I looked at what time he sent the message, it was minutes after Brooke called me. To be honest I don't want to know about them for today, I will enjoy the time I have with my cousins, they will stay a few days and I almost never see them. The others were waking up one by one. Everyone on the phone but with the company that was closest. That is until an aunt came.

"*Ya levantense flojos!* Come to eat."

We got up, the boys went out first and we took our time to make ourselves presentable. I didn't want to change and I stayed in my pajamas, I put on my bra and went to brush my teeth, then I brushed my hair and went out. The last ones were my sister and the annoying cousin.

She asks, "What are we going to eat?"

"*Frijoles con huevo*" She makes a bad face and I resist trying to say that she better do something or that she better not even eat.

My uncle, her dad, quickly told her to sit down, "Come on, sit down."

She complains about what they give her as if she were a princess but she is not, payasa.

She continues with her *fuchi* face but everyone at the table ignores her, I know that bothered her even more but it doesn't matter. We all had breakfast in peace, and my cousins were planning what to do during these days.

Chapter 15

JASMINE

"Matias, be careful! You are going to…" And it falls epically. "Fall," we all approached to see how he was.

Matias gets up and shakes himself. "I'm fine, I'm fine, I just scraped my knee."

My cousin Karla tells him, "That will surely leave a scar."

"It better leave one, right?" We all laughed at what he said.

We had gotten bored at home and we went out to entertain ourselves in the street. One of my cousins brought a skateboard and some skates and we decided to ride them but it should be noted that almost no one knows how to use them.

Not all of us were here, my sister stayed with the other *pariente* to "not leave her alone" but I know it's to keep an eye on her, sometimes she gets out of hand and decides to grab things for herself. My things or my sister's, even my mom's!

Matias makes sure he is okay and continues using the skateboard. I tried to use the skates but at the first attempt I almost fell.

My cousin Natalia yells, "Come on Jasmine, you can do it!"

"Shut up, don't yell."

I got up again but this time alone, the first few seconds went well but then I lost control, I heard my cousins yelling at me "Be careful!" but I couldn't stop, I didn't have to grab to stop and without warning I crashed with someone causing us to fall and me on top of the person.

With all the shame in the world I apologized, "I apologize with all my heart." I didn't want to look him in the face.

"There's no reason, *Boneca*." I would know that voice anywhere and that nickname was only told to me by one person.

I said looking at his face, "I wouldn't know whether to be surprised that you're here or not."

"Good thought." I get off him but I fall backwards trying to get up. "Careful, let me help you." Whether I want to or not, I lean on him.

My cousins came running towards us and they saw that I was fine and calmed down a little. They saw Thiago and how he was hugging me so I didn't fall. With a gesture I tried to tell my cousin to make her understand that I'll talk to her later.

"Well, thanks but I have to go." I separated from him and a cousin helped me.

With a smile he says, "No problem." I notice how my cousins see him as trying to intimidate him. How funny.

I almost forgot that they are like my brothers and well, they are somewhat protective.

I took off the skates and put on my shoes, we grabbed our things and then went home, it was already late, right now it could be considered the golden hour. Everything looks very pretty and my cousins take the opportunity to take photos.

"*Ay que tomarnos una foto para el Facebook.*" they got together and took about a thousand photos. "Jasmine, come!" I approached and got in the back.

I don't really like taking pictures of myself, I always go wrong or something comes out that makes it look bad. I'm a bit chubby and sometimes the photos take the angle that I don't like.

The photo that she decided to publish doesn't show my body, just a bit where my collarbones go, my face looks very round and I don't like it but I didn't want to say anything about it. We were close to the house, we were talking but we stopped when we saw how Cristina— the annoying cousin—was talking with someone on the phone.

My cousin Karla and I looked at each other, I knew they wanted to listen to the conversation; we approached the truck that was parked in front of the house and hid to listen.

"I didn't want to come but my dad forced me, I wanted to go with my mom... nothing to do with them, they are unbearable..." I bet my twenty dollars that she was talking about us. "A party? Where?... I know they won't let me go but I can escape for one night." She says it as if it were the most normal thing in the world! "Ok bye." She hangs up and enters the house.

"Should we do something or that she alone gets into trouble?"

"We could make her the *maldad* of accusing her but I don't know."

I would just ignore her.

"And if better, let's see that party?" Says a cousin and we all turn to see him. "What? *Solo digo*. We could meet guys, that's my humble opinion."

We entered the house and everyone went to do their thing, well, except for Karla, she immediately took me to the room and I know why she is doing this, she closes the door and while I get the idea of what she will ask me.

"Who was he?"

"My friend."

"Why did he hold you like that?"

"I fell and he helped me."

"How long have you known each other?"

"Not that long, a few days."

"Are you and him dating?"

"Nope."

"Sleeping?"

"Fuck no."

"*Esta chulo.*"

"*Lo se.*"

Karla stared at me for a few minutes and then we laughed, ever since she gave me that look in the park I knew she would fill me with questions, I knew she wouldn't be left alone with doubts.

"Where is he from? From a distance you can tell that he is not a *gringo*."

She asks something I've also wanted to know, "Honestly, I don't even know, but I do know that he speaks Portuguese."

"*De verdad?* So he must be from Portugal." At that moment, really, I wanted to slap her at her face.

"Dear *prima*, let me tell you that there are other places where they speak the same language."

She realizes what she said and says, "Oh, yes, true."

After talking a bit about other things, we decided to leave the room but when we opened the door we saw Cristina enter my sister's room, we looked at each other and immediately we approached to the door; Cristina was looking in the closet. Everyone here knows that she doesn't like to mix her clothes so there's no reason for her to be looking through my sister's clothes.

I didn't hold back and I called her attention, "What do you think you're doing?" As expected, she was surprised.

"Nothing you care about."

"Stop rummaging through Vanessa's things, your clothes are in your suitcase, do you also want me to tell you where it is?" I was treating her like a little girl and I know she doesn't like that.

"Could you just go!"

"Only if you go first." I was acting calm, there was no reason to be acting like a scared cat like her.

We both sent each other looks that if the looks hit each other we would have scratches and bruises all over our bodies, especially our faces.

It annoys me that sometimes they don't do anything to punish her, they just say things like "let it go" "she won't do it again". My ass!

I made fists with my hands, I think that the fact that she is not taking me seriously only makes me more angry.

We looked at each other for a while without saying anything, Karla didn't say anything either but she remained alert. Cristina sees me from head to toe and smiles mockingly.

She did not.

Chapter 16

JASMINE

"I'm not to blame for anything! She pushed me first and of course I pushed her back!" I said—yelled—while I put ice on my eye.

"Liar!" Cristina says while her dad cleans the scratch I gave her on her arm.

"I don't care who did what, these are not ways to fix things and you Jasmine, you should know how to behave." I really didn't believe what my mom was telling me.

"So I'm the one being scolded here?! She was *esculcando* through Vanessa's clothes, and everyone here knows that she didn't take her clothes out of her suitcase!"

My mom doesn't listen to me and continues defending her, "She was just looking for a *fajo mija*, that's nothing."

"If it was nothing then SHE wouldn't have pushed me and punched me in the face! LOOK HOW SHE LEFT MY EYE!" I took off the ice and looked at my mom with anger.

When I kindly asked Cristina to leave the room, she pushed me on the way out and that made me crash into the door frame. Of course, I pushed her back and then she started throwing punches, she hit me in the eye and now it's turning purple. A bad purple.

I scratched her and I'm sure that would leave a few small scars. My parents and my uncles heard us and separated us, Karla held me while my sister held that *escuincla*.

"You are already adults, you should behave as such."
Ma, which side are you on?

Cristina did not remain silent and still tried to defend herself, "She is the one who misunderstood what I was doing, she attacked me first!" She is very good at acting and I know that some here will believe her.

Then my mom said something that really made me angry. "Jasmine, go and finish the chores."

"What?! Why?!" I noticed how Crustina smiled maliciously. "If you think I'm acting like a child, why don't you keep an eye on this cat? She was planning to escape tonight to go to a party." Her face turned pale.
Take that bitch.

"Stop making things up." My mom was really taking her side and not mine, her daughter.

"*Ma...*" Vanessa tried to call her but she didn't pay attention.

"Well, you don't want to believe me, well I'll give you the luxury of not seeing this 'liar' of a daughter." I got up and left the house.

The day was supposed to end peacefully with a delicious dinner and talking to each other, not in a fight in which the wrong is accused.

I walked and walked until I reached the park that is close to the school, it is a little far away but I really didn't care. Turkey week is supposed to be about giving thanks for everything we receive and have.

Am I supposed to be thankful about the family I have even if my own mother doesn't stand up for me?

It is difficult to think about these types of situations, my dad is not one to talk much but he did not speak during the entire time we argued and I would have appreciated it if he said at least something, my sister tried but she has never had to deal with this side of my mother but I did.

I sat on a swing and there I was without swinging, I realized that I didn't bring my phone or any money, it's starting to get cold and I don't even have a sweater. I think it was around twelve or almost one.

I wanted to cry, I had a nod in my throat and it was difficult for me to swallow saliva, this type of feeling is the worst and sometimes I have these types of episodes but I don't tell anyone. My sister would worry and she already has enough stress with college, my mom doesn't believe in those things about anxiety or depression, she thinks it's just to get attention.

My dad... not the best person to talk about that I would say.

I don't want to go back but I don't have anywhere else to go either.

I don't know what will happen if I return, most likely they will make me apologize to that... to Cristina but I wouldn't do it, I have my pride and some dignity, I wouldn't leave it on the ground for something that I know I did well. Well, maybe fighting wasn't the best option but at least I didn't initiate it.

It started to get windy, I think it was time to go back, I'll see if the window in my room is open.

I started walking and while I was rubbing my arms to get rid of the cold a little, I looked everywhere. I think it was also stupid to have gone out without anything to protect myself. I arrived at my street, the house was still with the lights on, I guess they were waiting for me.

I went to my window and luckily for me it was open, I carefully put one leg in and then the other, I went in completely and when I turned I saw that there was Karla and Matias on their phones, they looked up and saw me. The three of us wanted to laugh but I put my finger in my mouth to make them shut up.

After a few minutes she asked, "Are you okay?"

"No..."

"We explained to our uncles about what we heard in her conversation on the phone, she became hysterical because we 'invaded' her privacy, her father *la regaño* and forced her to apologize to your parents and then they punished her." Says Matias. I listened attentively but even if he said that, it doesn't make me completely fine.

"Well, bad for her, she deserved it."

We stayed talking for a while longer but it was time to sleep. The others who were sleeping in my room came in and saw me and hugged me, well, they crushed me. I also asked them not to say I was here, I know it will worry my mom more but the truth is that I don't want to have to talk to her, at least not right now.

I didn't sleep the rest of the night.

I grabbed my phone and stayed watching videos. I looked at the time every now and then to know how much more time I had left before I could fall asleep but it didn't come. I left the application where I was and went to messages, I looked at his contact and mentally debated whether to send him a message or not. I don't think he's awake, after all it's five in the morning. Unless he's someone with insomnia or just likes to stay up late doing things, who knows.

I tried to get comfortable in my bed, I moved about six or seven times and I couldn't find the position I wanted. The worst of all is that I don't know what I want.

Chapter 17

THIAGO

I was satisfied to have been able to see her, when she left with her cousins I returned to my house. What happened today was not a coincidence, I knew that she went out today and was just looking for where she was, of course, her falling was not part of the plan but the good thing was that I was able to help her.

I was busy all day and I was stressed but seeing her helped me a little. When I returned home I continued with what I was doing, I had to make sure my "business" wasn't out of control. I made call after call and sent some messages, I even called Brooke, leaving aside the issue of Jasmine, we still have work pending.

"What do you mean he didn't send us the money? Why?"
"Because according to him, the work did not turn out as he expected."
"What do you mean no?! I myself made sure that his documents were out of the police system, the police! Fuck!"
"I know, we can still do what I have in mind if he doesn't send the money by tomorrow."

"I don't know, that's too much."
"Aha, of course. Well, how about a warning?"
"Alright."

Even though we both don't like each other, business is something we don't stop doing, we do jobs for other people and we receive money for it, nothing we do is legal and something may go wrong but it's like a drug, once you feel the adrenaline of having done something wrong, you just want to feel it again.

Somehow I have to get money.

> "By the way, today I was curious to enter the camera on Jasmine's phone and before you give me shit, there is something I noticed that I didn't like." I looked at the screen of my phone—I had it on speaker—confused.
> "What are you talking about?"
> "Well, first of all, she didn't have it with her, apparently she left it in her room or in something of hers; second, it was after 10 and from what I could hear she was not at home."
> "How strange, she never goes out without her phone."
> "I know."
> "Wait a minute, how do you know she never leaves her phone?!"
> "*Eu te perguntaria a mesma coisa!*"
> "Don't give me that, don't ask me how I know because I'm more of her friend than you!"
> "*Eu também sou seu amigo!*"

Sometimes I hate the fact that he knows how to speak Portuguese. We left that topic aside to continue with what we were doing, there were still things undone. 20 minutes later we finished and hung up the call. I leaned back in the chair and closed my eyes for a moment.

Not a second passed and I heard a notification arrive. I look at my phone and see that it is a message, I grab my phone and see who it is, I was a little surprised but I answered.

'Are you awake?' I was going to reply but the message was immediately deleted.

'For your luck, yes, yes I am.'

'I didn't wake you up, did I?' I get up and go to bed.

'No, is something wrong? You should be asleep by now.' Why would she be awake so early in the morning?

'I'm not sleepy.' I know something's up, no one is awake just because. 'Why are you awake?'

'I'm not sleepy.' I bet whatever, that using the same words as hers made her smile.

'I'm not sleeping because something happened here at home and it doesn't let me stay calm, I won't go into details but it's that bad.'

So something did happen.

'I understand, but you should try to sleep, it's the best way to escape reality.'

'You're right, well, then good night.'

'Good night.'

I should find out what happened. She left her phone at her house and she never leaves it anywhere. If she forgets, she comes back in a matter of minutes. How do I know that detail? I'll just say that I have a lot of free time.

I went to sleep after looking at a photo of her for a few minutes.

JASMINE

I looked out the window as the sun began to rise, I didn't sleep, I couldn't. When I said "good night" to Thiago, I downloaded a game and played all night. I got up and went to the bathroom, when I came out I went to see if anyone else had woken up, it's six in the morning so I think not yet.

I went to the kitchen and saw everything ready for cooking today. It's the 23rd and it's turkey day. I always accompany the family at the table and I'm grateful for what I have but I know it will be uncomfortable to be sitting there after what happened.

I went back to the room and grabbed some clothes. I'll take a quick shower. Ready, I left the room and went to the kitchen, I was hungry, after all I couldn't have dinner last night.

I got to the kitchen but to my bad luck, my mother was there with an aunt, they were talking. I decided to listen to them.

My aunt asks, "Don't you think you were a little harsh? Jasmine looked sad."

My mom, very convinced she says, "*Esa niña* knows that she should behave when there are visitors, do you think that if some of your children behaved like that in another house, would you let them be? Jasmine is already 19 years old, she should behave as such."

"No, but we're among family, and also," my aunt gets a little closer to my mom and whispers to her. "You know how Cristina is, she's always had a long hand. Besides, the others already explained to us how the matter was."

Finally someone who sees things as they are!

"Leave it like that, Jasmine is sure she's just doing this to annoy me." Me? bother her? For what?

My aunt asks confused, "Why do you say that?"

"Because the other time Victor's family came, I scolded her because her cousins told me that she was hanging out with that boy who I told you was released from prison." *Pero que chingados?*

"But what's wrong with it?"

Aunt, I love that you are not a judgy person!

"*Ay ya!* Let's do it and help me with the salad."

So my mom thinks that's why I "behave" like that. What nonsense, really. In that case, if that's what she believes then there's no point in joining them for dinner.

I went back to my room and grabbed a backpack. This time I will carry things to be able to survive outside. I'm not going to escape but

I won't stay here enduring all this either. Matias woke up and looked at me confused, I put my finger to my lips so he would stay quiet.

"I'll just be outside, don't worry, I'll be back at night." He nods, not very convinced.

Having my things ready, I went out the window. The first thing I did was go to a cafe. I have to eat something. I went in and approached a table that was next to the window, the waitress came over and asked me for my order.

She says with a smile, "Good morning, what do you want to order?"

"Morning, a coffee and a waffle, and could I have some fruit on the side?"

"Of course, I'll bring it to you in a moment."

"Thank you."

Who knew I would be having breakfast out and not at home?

I wanted to cry, this really wasn't fair. I rubbed my eyes to stop myself from letting out a tear, what a shame to cry in public. I took a few breaths to calm down, my eye is hurting.

Minutes later the waitress brought me my order and I ate.

The day looks beautiful, it is a little windy and in some trees you can see the change of colors. You can see the orange, yellow and even a few red leaves. I always liked the colors of this season.

The day started badly but I really hope it doesn't get worse, I have a limit to being able to put up with this type of thing and I don't want to reach that line.

Chapter 18

JASMINE

After having breakfast I left without knowing what to do, I didn't want to go to the park, I didn't want to go to the mall—I wouldn't buy anything anyway—, and much less I wanted to return.

I want to scream... loudly.

I decided to just walk, I had no other choice.

I stopped at a gas station, I was getting hungry. It was already after twelve so yes, I had to eat something. First I went and got some orange juice, then I got some chips, and finally I went to see what kind of sandwiches they had.

"The turkey one looks good but I'm craving one with salami."

I heard someone say my name, "Jasmine?" I looked to my sides and looked at Thiago, he had some bags of chips in his hands and some soda.

I said a little nervous, "Thiago, hi"

"I didn't expect to see you here," he says with a confused expression. "Is the store on our street closed?"

"Ah, I don't know, why?"

I think it was strange to find myself in a store that is far from my house when there is already a store nearby.

"Are you okay? You look tired."

Could it be because I haven't slept?

"I'm fine, don't worry."

Thiago didn't look very convinced, nor would I be if I saw someone with a tired face like me. Before leaving the bathroom, I looked in the mirror, I had dark circles and my eyes were a little red, and my eye looked very purple so I had to cover it with makeup. I wanted to tell him that I had gotten into a fight with my mom and that I was avoiding being home, but I didn't want to overwhelm him with my problems.

"Are you sure? Does it have to do with the 'little' problem that happened at your house?" I had forgotten that I told him that.

"Well it could be."

He says with his face a little more relaxed, "Do you need to talk, or some company?"

"I think so…"

It's a good thing he didn't notice the makeup.

We both continued walking, I noticed that we were going back, I was going to tell him that I didn't want to go back but we stopped at his house, I realized that he wanted me to come in.

"My parents are not here, and I don't think they will be back soon."

"I don't want to bother." The truth is that it gets on my nerves just thinking about being alone with him.

I have never had a partner, I have not had my first kiss, I have done absolutely nothing. It doesn't scare me but I've never even been in the room of a boy who isn't a family member.

He says with a small smile,"You're not bothering at all." A sincere one.

I accepted and entered his house, he immediately apologized for the mess in the living room, there were many empty alcohol bottles and cigarette packs. We went up stairs and I could notice the difference. Up here it was much cleaner and there was no trash lying around, I guess his parents don't go up here.

We stopped in front of a door and he opened it, he let me in and the first thing I saw was a computer with four monitors.

"Sit wherever you like, there is a sofa if you want to sit there," he says while pointing to it.

"Thank you."

He says after a few minutes, "Do you want to tell me what happened?"

"I don't want to bother you with my problems."

"Come on, you'll feel better." One way or another I have to vent.

I started to tell him about when my other family came to visit, I told him about the scolding that my mother gave me and then I jumped to where what happened with Cristina, I told him about how she is, about how she does what she wants and whenever she wants, and the things she does behind her dad. I got to the point where I fought with her, I noticed how he tensed up and he almost moved his arms as if he wanted to tell me something, but he stopped, and I continued.

I told him what I heard this morning and how I decided not to return until nightfall.

"Can I see your eye? You have to ensure that it is healing."

"Sure, can I go to your bathroom?"

"Yes, is the left door."

I got up and took my backpack, took out a makeup remover wipe and cleaned myself carefully, it still hurt. When I took off my makeup, I wet my eye a little with cold water and dried it with a towel that was there. When he left he was on his phone, sending a message, I think.

He realized that I came out and he saw me, well he saw my eye. He got up and stood in front of me, put his hand on my chin and made me lift my face.

"It's not as bad as it looks."

"I know you're lying, *Boneca.*"

Thiago is too close, I don't know what I should do, should I separate or stay still and wait for what could happen?

"It hurts but I can bear it."

He doesn't respond, he doesn't say anything, he just stays there. I feel how he slides his hand up slowly giving me chills. Thiago gets even closer if that's possible , he puts his hand on my waist and when I think he's about to kiss me, a scream is heard from outside.

I immediately separate myself from him and take a few breaths.

At what point did I stop breathing?

I can see how he got upset and he went to look out the window. He curses and rubs his eyes. Without saying anything he opens the door and leaves.

Was he about to kiss me? And I was going to let him do it?! No, it was for the moment, yes, yes it was for that. But wouldn't that be worse?

I hear someone start shouting so I go to the window and I really can't believe who was there shouting at Thiago. I was going to get his attention but I heard a noise, I looked at one of the monitors and saw that a message had arrived.

Curiosity killed the cat... but satisfaction brought him back.

Chapter 19

BROOKE

I was taking a shower when I received a notification on my computer. When I left, I wrapped a towel around my waist and went over to see what it was. It's from Thiago's room. Some time ago, he asked me to place a system on his computer where the camera would detect a second person, for protection.

I clicked on the notification and swore at that moment that I would kill him. I got dressed as quickly as I could, grabbed the keys and got into my car. I drove as fast as I could, I didn't care if they gave me tickets, I just cared about getting to that bastard's house.

When I arrived, I tried to open the door but of course it was closed, but I started screaming. To be able to get his attention.

"GET OUT YOU SON OF A BITCH! THIAGO!" Seconds later he looked out the window and I could see the anger in him.

I will castrate him, I don't care about the legal issues, I swear I will castrate him.

The door opened immediatcly with him shouting, "What the hell do you want?!"

"I think you forgot that I can see through your camera dear Thiago." At first, he seems not to know what I'm talking about but then he gets it.

"Fuck... Anyway, you don't have the damn right to come and invade my house."

"What the hell were you trying to do to Jasmine? Uh? Answer me!"

He was going to answer me, but we heard a loud sound, we both turned to see what it was. It was Jasmine who opened the door with force and got out of the house.

"Jasmine?" When I spoke to her she looked at me with a scared face, that hurt me. "What's wrong? Did he do something to you?"

I was about to complain to Thiago, but he also looked confused. I separated from him and tried to get closer to Jasmine, but she backed away.

"Jasmine?" Thiago also spoke to her but it was the same with him.

She gave us one last look and ran away. I wanted to go after her but something tells me I shouldn't. We both look at each other, without knowing what to do.

I asked, "What happened? Why did she act like that?"

Says Thiago, still annoyed, "I don't know, we were fine before you arrived." But I no longer gave importance to that—later I complained to him—now what I had in mind is to know why Jasmine was scared.

"Did you say anything to her about us?"

"No, not at all." I see how his expression suddenly changed. "Shit." He says before running back into the house.

I didn't hesitate to follow him. I entered the house and went up the stairs. I got to his room and saw that he was staring at his monitors. I got a little closer to have a better view and there I understood Jasmine's behavior.

"Shit, shit, shit. Jasmine read the message and saw the photos."

"What photos?" He doesn't respond. "Thiago, what photos?"

"She looked at the photos of the body from the last physical work we did, photos to confirm the work.. The body is full of blood and you are carrying it and I think she also saw the video where I am burying it."

"Damn it!" This shouldn't happen, not like this.

I was going to leave the room, I had to go with her so I could explain the situation better, Jasmine should not have found out about this, not this way! Thiago stopped me by grabbing my arm.

"Wait, she's not at her house." I looked at him confused.

"How come she's not at her house? What are you talking about?"

"I won't go into details because it's not something I have the right to tell you, but she is not at her house because she had a problem with her family."

"What a problem?"

"I won't tell you, understand!"

If he doesn't tell me then it's something serious. But I wasn't going to let this stay like this. I left the house and decided to look for her. I didn't know where to start, she could be everywhere. I took out my phone and made some calls. I will have all my contacts look for her.

JASMINE

I shouldn't have seen that message. I shouldn't have seen those photos. I shouldn't have seen the video. I shouldn't have gotten involved with them.

As soon as I looked at what was on the monitor, I knew I had to leave the house immediately and never come back, I knew I had to get away from the two of them and imagine that I almost kissed him. This is too much to process. I knew that Thiago was in prison, but I thought it was for robbery or violence but not for... not for murder.

Returning home was not the best option, what would I say to my mother if she saw me so upset? I can't go to the police, what am I supposed to tell them?

Those messages were from that moment, that means that they are both active, since when have they been doing that?

I got to the public library, I'll hide there while I can, I'll see what to do next. I entered and smiled at the librarian; I went to the depths of the place. While I was looking for where to sit, I remembered what I had seen weeks ago, I didn't imagine it, it really happened, Thiago really killed someone in his room... and I witnessed him.

Am I a witness?! An accomplice?!

I shouldn't be involved in this.

I found a corner that looked cozy. I sat on the floor and couldn't take it anymore and started crying, this was overwhelming me. This isn't a story where I overlook something like this, what am I supposed to do? I'm fighting with my family, and I don't want to see them. I can't go with those I thought were my friends, I don't have anyone. Brooke and Thiago are murderers... why were they interested in talking to me in the first place?

Were they planning to kill me?

That simple thought gave me chills. I know I wanted something exciting to happen to me, but why this?

Que hago? Que hago? Que hago?

Chapter 20

JASMINE

I had fallen asleep but the librarian woke me up, and I was still on the floor. I thanked and left the place. I looked at the time.

6:47 PM

It's late and I'm hungry. I looked around before walking, I was very alone which made me nervous. For a Wednesday afternoon it looked very lonely; I kept walking until I reached the mall. I wanted a milkshake and I like the ones they sell there.

While asking, I remembered that I had spent part of the afternoon there with Brooke, I wanted to cry but I didn't, I'll have to get the idea that I won't have that type of encounter with him or Thiago again. The man gave me my drink and I went to sit at one of the tables.

"Miss Santos?" Someone said my last name and I looked up.

It's a man... a big man dressed in a jacket and black glasses. I got up quickly from my chair, I was about to run away but he put aside his jacket and showed me a knife, a big one.

"W-what do you want?" I had a trembling voice, I could barely speak.

"I don't want to cause a fuss, okay? Follow me and everything will be fine."

Pues, does this guy think I was born yesterday?

"I don't want to, please let me go." I was already on the verge of tears.

He says with a harsher voice, "Miss, please come with me."

I didn't want to think that this had to do with the two of them, but what else would it be? My family is not rich, I am not important, who in their right mind would want to kidnap me? And in broad daylight! I'm nobody.

The man was still here, he was still waiting for me and I didn't know what to do. I could try to run away but there is a high possibility that he will catch me and kill me instantly.

"Come with me, he wants to see you and he is worried about you."

I wanted to ask him which of the two, but what do I gain by knowing who? I had no choice but to follow him. I stood up straight and waited for him to start walking, he understood, and I stood next to him. We both started walking.

We were just a few meters away from leaving the mall but I looked at a guard, I thought about whether it would be worth the risk to go with him or should I attract the attention of that guard. I didn't know what to do, all this was clouding my mind and I couldn't think clearly.

Will I die if I try escaping?

I was sitting on a sofa with a bottle of water in my hand, I was nervous, I moved my foot non-stop and I honestly don't know if I did the right thing. There were few people in the place, they walked from one place to the other doing who knows what. I already wanted to go but I knew I had to wait a little longer.

The majority here were men, there were only a few women. Everyone had a gun at their side and that made me nervous just by seeing it.

"Jasy." I heard my name and I looked at him, there he was.

"What do you want from me?" I was afraid, I didn't want anything to happen to me.

"No, I don't want you to think like that," he says, putting himself to my height. "I want to explain things to you, I want you not to look at me with those eyes," he says with a little desperation in his voice.

"How do you want me to see you then? Brooke, you are a murderer." Saying that made me want to cry, I felt a drop fall on one of my hands. "Or are you going to deny it to me? I saw the messages and the photos, even a video! Fuck." I rub my face with exasperation.

Brooke didn't say anything, he knew I was right. There's no way he could see this any other way.

What if I'm still his friend? Ignoring the fact that he's killed someone? Will it be worth it?

Neither of us spoke, what were we going to say? I don't know what to do, all this is too much. I tried not to look at his face, I looked everywhere except his face, his eyes; It was a bad idea though, because at the door where Brooke had entered before, Thiago was leaning against the door frame.

He looked towards us, his eyes were empty, there was no emotion in them.

Brooke noticed where I was looking, he let out a sigh and stood up. He looked at him and he approached, Thiago didn't look at me, he didn't say anything, he just stayed there silently.

I said almost in a whisper, "I want to go home."

"Jasy…"

"I said I want to go home now."

The day had already ended, Thanksgiving came to an end, and what followed were normal days. I know I will be uneasy at home but I have no other choice.

"Okay, I'll take you."

"I can go alone." I got up from the chair and walked towards the exit. I passed by Thiago but there was no reaction.

I guess after all I never had the friends I thought I had. I feel like an idiot for believing that I was going to finally have a group friend. Childish from me.

I left the place, I was at Brooke's house, I had never been here before but realized that it was not very far from the school. I walked until I reached my house, I stood in front of the door looking at it for a few minutes, it's almost midnight and I don't know how my parents will react. There was only one way to find out.

I opened the door and everything fell silent, everyone was in the living room, my mom was on the couch, I noticed that her eyes were red, my dad was next to her, and everyone else was spread out, looking at me.

"Jasmine!" says my mom, getting up quickly to hug me. "*Ay hija,* I'm so sorry, please never go out like that again." I clung to her.

I said with a broken voice, "Sorry, *mami.*"

My dad also got up and hugged me tightly, I couldn't take it anymore and I started to cry very hard. I cried for everything, for my stupid cousin, for having spent this day without my family, for having believed in two damned people and for having been stupid.

I apologized to them as much as I could. My mom and I stayed hugging until dawn, we didn't speak, words were unnecessary. I relaxed and fell asleep like when I was a child, when I had a nightmare and I went to her so she could tell me that they were just things in my imagination and that it wouldn't hurt me.

After having these very stressful days, I was finally able to relax a little. But even though I was giving myself this moment I also realized that I no longer have anyone, I don't have Brooke and I don't have Thiago.

Chapter 21

JASMINE

It's been a month since I discovered what they did. When we returned to class I avoided talking to Brooke at all costs, the first few days he did everything to be able to talk to me but after a while he stopped, I did nothing but focus on my studies. Mindy kept trying to talk to him but it stayed the same and she still thinks it's because of me.

On the other hand, Thiago, I didn't see him again, neither in the store nor on the street, but I still ignored that fact. I didn't go to the police to accuse them, I know I should have done it but I didn't want that pressure on my chest, I didn't want to be thinking that it was my fault they were both locked up.

Right now I was accompanying Vanessa to a store because in a few days it's her boyfriend's birthday. She hasn't asked me questions about my suddenly lonely life, I know she realized that I no longer talk to the "friends" I had and I'm grateful that she gave me the space, anyway, I wouldn't know what to say to her.

"Do you think he would like this one?" she says as she holds up a knitted sweater with a pine tree in the middle.

"I've only known him for two months and he's with you most of the time, so don't ask me things I don't know."

"True, I think I'll start bringing you when I have dates with him."

"*Ni loca.*" We both laughed and continued looking.

I told Vanessa that I was hungry and we went to a small food place that had just opened. We entered and a waiter served us.

"Good morning ladies, here is the menu." He gave us the folder and left.

My sister asked, "Can I ask you a question?" She had a serious face.

"Yeah."

"I know that maybe you don't want to talk about it because of how you've been acting, but what happened to that friend of yours?" I stayed silent, I didn't know what to answer.

She didn't get to know Brooke because I only talked to him at school and on the phone. She knew about Thiago—but not in person—because I went out with him a while ago. I know she is asking about him, but what am I supposed to tell her? I looked at Vanessa, she looked at me with concern, since I was little I had never been good at having friends, yes, I had one or another but they never lasted around me.

"I had a fight with him, that's all."

"And there is no way to solve it? I know it's been a while but you looked happier when you talked to him."

Can it be resolved?

"Well ladies, do you know what you are going to order?"

We ordered the food and continued talking, but about something else. The food arrived and we ate in silence, a few words but most of the time in silence. While we were eating I could see how the waiter stared at my sister. I don't blame him, Vanessa has an energy that attracts people. When we finished we returned to the house. Along the way she continued to complain because she couldn't find a gift for her boyfriend.

We passed by his house, I couldn't help but look out the window, I do miss him and I even think I could have come to like him if we had kissed. But things happen for a reason just as they don't happen.

When we got home, we saw my mom talking to one of her friends. We said hello and everyone went their own way, well not before Vanessa told me that later I would accompany her to eat with Owen—Vanessa's boyfriend—to "get to know him better."

I think the relationship is serious.

I went into my room and closed the door. There are two days left until Christmas but in a few hours we will go to New Mexico to spend Christmas and New Years. We planned to go just by ourselves but my sister talked to my parents and now it will be a trip together with Owen's family. We will go by car and it is a thirteen hour trip so the earlier the better.

It's barely nine in the morning and I already want to go back to sleep, Vanessa had woken me up early. I lay in bed looking at the ceiling, after thinking about it for a long time I put up posters about things I wanted to do in my life, things I wanted to do before I died. There are many things but there is still more.

I grabbed a backpack and started packing things that I would use to entertain myself during the trip. I packed two books, a word search book, a pencil bag, my phone charger and headphones, and some chips. I left the room and went to the living room, I had to get some bottles of water.

"Well, I have to go, see you later," the lady says, getting up.

"Yes, see you later, when we get back maybe we can make dinner." Did I hear what I hear? My mom accompanied the lady to the door.

I asked just as she closed the door, "What dinner are you talking about?"

"*Jesus*, she invited us to her house to eat but I told her about the trip and *quedamos* that, after the trip."

But why that lady?! I know her bad intentions, she wants me for her son, Chihuahua!

We all have our things ready, the suitcases are already in the truck and my dad was making sure everything was closed. We left the house and got into the truck, while my dad turned it on I got comfortable. I put on my most comfortable pajama pants I had and a black sleeveless top—I'm not very confident about my body but there are times when I don't care and I wear whatever I want—, some slippers and I brought a blanket. I took out my headphones and put them on.

I put on my favorite playlist and the trip began.

Minutes later we left the city, then the atmosphere became more relaxed. I like the city but if I had to live in a place for life without having to worry about anything, I would go to live in a house in the country, around trees, flowers and wild animals.

I decided to sleep first, I'll do whatever when I wake up.

Chapter 22

THIAGO

I can not take this. I can't stand it. I can't see her, not like this. The fear in her eyes is not something I want to see, much less it was me who caused that in her. I wasn't supposed to hurt her, I wouldn't hurt her... but I did.

When she left Brooke's house, I wanted to turn back time and ignore Brooke and stay with her. Having kissed her for the first time. I could see her fear in her eyes, she was afraid of me.

Jasmine left the house and a while later she passed by again, I looked at her as much as I could but I was where she couldn't see me. I know she looked out the window, but I know she didn't want to see me. It was already noon when I decided to go out and try my luck to see if I could see her, even if it was just for a second. When I reached the corner, I looked at her dad loading things into the truck and my whole body stayed still.

Are they moving?! Will she leave?!

I also looked at her mother carrying things, I wanted to get closer but it would be risky. Minutes later everyone came out and got on, she was dressed comfortably. I know she doesn't notice it but she has curves that I would love to feel, to see everyday.

I breathed easier when I noticed that they didn't have all their things, maybe they were going out, after all it won't be long until it's Christmas, if none of this had happened we might have had our first Christmas together.

The truck passed and I was on the side where I could see her, she had put on her headphones and settled in, she didn't see me and I had the small hope that she would, I know it's the least she would want to do but I was dying for her to see me again. There I stood until I lost sight of the truck. I don't know where she is going but I hope she has fun.

"Thiago you should leave her alone."

"You know it's impossible, I'm not you, I won't give up, I'll wait until she's ready to see me again and we can talk again."

"It will take time," Brooke says, standing next to me.

"I know."

After what happened we continued doing jobs, even if I wanted to I couldn't let so much shit walk in the same place as her, Jasmine deserves to walk through a clean city. I know that Brooke tried to talk to her as best he could but as expected, it didn't work. The exact reason Brooke is here is because we have a job to do, and she happens to be dealing with the neighbor across the street.

How does that pig live near her?

I put on my gloves and a mask, then Brooke does it and we enter the house

We entered without a problem, no one noticed so it was easy. We closed the windows and doors and turned off the lights while we searched for him, the place became darker and if that man noticed, he would leave on his own and it would be easy to take care of him.

I entered a room that was dark, he was watching TV, Brooke came in and we both surprised him. He began to choke him with a cable and I stabbed his throat with a blade. His blood began to come out quickly. I positioned him in such a way that when they found him, they would think it was an accident. They may be suspicious because of the mark left by the cable, but I doubt they will want to go deeper into the case after they discover his background.

We left through the back door and made sure everything was just as we left it. We got to the park and sat on a bench, we weren't expecting anything, we just decided to sit.

"Mindy has something against Jasmin, but she's getting serious," Brooke says out of nowhere.

"What are you talking about?" I asked confused, "and who the hell is Mindy?"

"Right, you don't know about her, she's a classmate from school and she's one of those girls who attract attention, they do anything for attention. Anyway, she can't stand being ignored and that's what Jasy has been doing and I think she's up to something."

"What makes you think that?"

"I hacked her computer and believe me, there are no pretty things there. A few days ago I went in and found a conversation she had with other girls and it happened that Mindy started telling them that Jasy talks about them and says a lot of bad things."

"What?!"

This is bad, very bad.

"I know. I will do what I can within the school but it won't be for long, whether I want it or not, that girl will do whatever it takes to make life impossible for her." He lets out a sigh as he finishes what he says.

I got up and went straight to my house, there was no need to say goodbye because I know that it won't be the only time I see him. When I arrived, I noticed that my parents were in the house, it's time to take the trash out. They just make a mess all over the house. I walked in and as I expected, they were both on the floor with cans of beer in their hands and a cigarette in the other.

"It's time for you to get out of here." They both saw me but ignored me, so I raised my voice. "I said get the hell out of my damn house!" The old man looks at me and gets up.

"You're not talking to me like that."

"I talk to you however I fucking want."

He raised his hand and was about to hit me but he had no chance. I pushed him to lose his balance a little and kicked him in the knee, he fell down in pain and my mother seems to regain consciousness and looks at her 'dear' husband on the ground.

"But what are you doing?!" She approaches him and tries to help him.

"You have until midnight to leave, enough time, if you don't leave by then I will make sure you leave without anything."

"How dare you!"

"This house is mine, remember?" She looks at me with hatred but that doesn't make me feel anything. I approach her face and tell her, "*Você criou isso, agora preste atenção nas consequências.*"

I grew up without the correct care, without the affection that a mother should give to her child. I am like this because of their irresponsibility and now they have to accept the results of their bad upbringing.

Chapter 23

JASMINE

I have already read both books for like the third time, I have already filled more than half of the word search and I have repeated my music more than five times—I can listen to my music a thousand more times, I have no problem with that—and Vanessa has been talking to her boyfriend for I don't know how many times and that's not counting the messages. We stopped to grab food and according to my mom that would be the last time.

I already want to arrive!

"Mother! How much is left?"

"One hour, almost there." Hallelujah!

The road itself was good, there were very nice views and we passed through some towns that looked nice. At the first stop we made, I bought snacks and drinks. I took photos of everything that caught my attention and so on. Several cute boys. Normal things to see on a trip.

I looked at the map on my cell phone and there were only a few minutes left. I started to feel excited, every time we can and we have enough money, we make these types of trips but it is not often. The last time we had a trip like this was when we went to the beach but in California. But I don't remember the place.

I get out of the truck and admire the beautiful cabin we are staying in this week. It's night and the lights make it look cozy. We entered the place—we collected the keys upon entering the place—and I was the first to look for the rooms. It was clear that the largest room was for my parents; I found one of the rooms and there was no need to go check on the other one.

The room was a good size and there was a full-length mirror, a wooden dresser that had floral decorations and things like that. It looked pretty.

I went out again and grabbed my things. I took my suitcase and backpack to the room. I took out some things and arranged them in the closet, I put the "essentials" on the table that was next to the bed, I put my charger, book, headphones and some snacks. Already ready and changed—because it is very cold—I went out to the back backyard; the snow made it look bright and spacious.

I got in and went to the kitchen, there was my mom and Owen's mom, the couple were in the living room taking photos. It turns out that Owen has a younger brother, Rafael. I didn't know he existed until I heard it from my sister when they were talking on the phone.

"Jas, go bring me the bag with the bread so we can all eat it soon," says my mom and I gladly get up because that means she will make hot chocolate.

I go out and look for the bag. I hear the door open and I see it's Rafael, I ignore him and continue looking for the bag, I don't know where my mom put it so it will be a little difficult. I went to the back and opened the trunk.

Someone speaks to me from behind, "Would you like me to help you?" and I turn to see who it is.

"Uh? If you want to." He smiles a little and starts searching.

Minutes later we found the bag. This was stuffed in a bag inside another, which was to be expected from my mom. I thanked him and we returned to the cabin, he went to do his things and I went to take bread to my mother.

"Did y'all talk?" is the first thing she says.

I ask confused, "Who?"

"You and the boy, did you talk?"

"*Ma'*, don't tell me that you sent him to go 'help' me just so we could talk?"

"Is that a no?" I can't believe it.

I left the kitchen and went to my room, since I won't be doing anything at the moment I decided to use my phone and see what I could find. There wasn't much on my social media but I found a video about an incident that happened in our neighborhood.

How strange, it's from just two hours ago.

"Today, December 23 at 11:20 at night, a lifeless body was found. The police discovered the inert body of Mr. Pedro Gamboa, it is said that apparently due to an accident he took his life but it is speculated that there is possibility of a murder, the doubts have not yet been clarified but they will take the case further."

"The body was found in his room, apparently he was watching TV and eating, the man took a bad step and with the knife that he had in his hand, he stabbed him through the throat. The officers say that he had marks on his throat, as if he had struggled with something but they don't know clearly..."

A murder?

I looked at the images that came with the video. I recognized the house and the street, it is right in front of my house, but how is it possible? That man was not a troublemaker, I always saw him watering his plants and sometimes he went out, he drank a lot but as far as I know, that was his only problem.

I saw the faces of those two, it was a fleeting memory but I tried not to think about it. Just because they already did it does not mean that they are responsible for this.

I left the phone on the bed, I should be having fun outside and not thinking about nonsense.

When I opened the door I got the smell of hot chocolate, with a smile I went to the kitchen and they were just serving it. My dad gave me a cup and I got in line. When my turn came, my mother served me and the lady gave me some *pan dulce*.

With my cup and bread in hand, I went to sit on the sofa, the table was already full—my dad, the lady's husband, my sister and her boyfriend had sat down and there were two more chairs for my mother and the lady—It was only Rafael and I left but he was sitting on another sofa.

I already missed something like this.

I was about to take a sip of my chocolate when I saw Rafael move, sitting next to me. Afterwards I felt watched. I looked at my mom, my sister and the lady looking at me.

Nope, this is not going to happen.

I ignored that fact and focused on what was important. I was on my phone the whole time, I didn't want to turn around or even smile at the boy because I felt like he was going to start a conversation and whether I wanted to or not, I didn't know how to start or continue a conversation.

The publications of that "accident" continued and continued, they still did not remove the idea that it was a murder but they have not been able to find anything, no evidence of that. I really hope that was it, a bad accident.

Chapter 24

JASMINE

I was in the truck looking for my gift bags, I had hidden them among the things so that my parents and my sister wouldn't see them. I had bought some things for Owen's family but I didn't bring anything for his brother, re-cap: I didn't even know he had a brother.

Having everything in hand, I returned to the cabin and went to my room. They saw me with the things but didn't ask questions; I left everything on my bed and grabbed my bag and my phone, I left and went to my mom.

"*Ma'*, can I go to the town? I want to go see the *tiendas*."

"Yes but not alone." She immediately saw Rafael.

"Vanessa, please come to the town with me," I said before my mom had a chance to ask him.

"Okay."

My mom didn't say anything for a second but then she said that it was fine and that we should be careful. We both left the cabin and walked, the town was not that far away.

When we arrived, the first thing we went to was to see the clothing stores, I looked where the men's shirts were, I wanted one for myself.

They are big, long and very comfortable. Sometimes my mom tells me to stop buying those clothes because they are for men.

I ended up buying two.

Vanessa and I went from store to store, she bought things for herself and a few things for her boyfriend. We arrived at a store where they sell keychains, stickers, bottles and more things. I grabbed some candy, a glass jar and other things. I was going to try to make the same gift as his family's but it would look a little different.

I already had everything ready, I just needed to put it in the gift bag. It's half past ten at night. The day was spent playing board games, eating, and chatting. My sister finally revealed to me that my mom is trying to get Rafael and me to get along, the reason? Because I look very lonely. After the fight we had and all the scandal, I didn't go out, not even to go to the store and the only times I went out were with her or my mom.

She noticed immediately that I don't have any friends, one time my mom asked me about Mindy and I explained to her that she had been behaving very badly and I decided to stay away from her.

We finished dinner and we all went to the living room to talk. My dad was talking about a hunt he did when he was young and he kept everyone entertained.

"My father at that time had told me, 'Don't be a chicken and get on the animal', clarifying that it was a deer that I couldn't knock down when I shot it."

Rafael says as he sits next to me, "Your dad has good stories."

"Yep, that's right." He was going to say something else but I realized that it was already eleven, so I called everyone, "It's time to put all the gifts in the fireplace." In the cabin there was no tree but there was a fireplace and we had said that that would be the space to put gifts.

I went to my room and grabbed all the gifts. For us, it is tradition to give gifts at midnight, that is how we receive Christmas; the *gringos* do it during the day but it is because of the belief in Santa Claus, and the children wait for the gifts to be there in the morning.

We all leave gifts, we all leave each other. There are no children and I feel like that makes it look a little more exciting, why do I think that? Because we always have to let them open the gifts first and sometimes they break the others and so on.

I got up from the floor—I was on the floor because I was arranging my bags so they wouldn't fall—and went to the kitchen, I wanted something to snack on. I searched the drawers and found nothing, then I searched the cabinets and found a package of cookies but they were high. I tried to stretch but I couldn't reach them.

I was about to jump when I saw a hand pass over me and grab the package, I turned around and saw that it was Rafael. He gave them to me and I thanked him, no one moved, we just stayed still. I noticed the position we were in, it was straight out of a book scene, I was against the island and he was in front of me, literally leaving me with no escape. He smiled at me.

I must admit that I got nervous.

The difference in height was big, I barely reached five feet and five inches, he looked much taller and I had to look up. He bends over and I lean back but there's not much I can do.

"I feel like you are avoiding me and I would like to know why." Am I avoiding him?

"I'm not avoiding you, now, if you allow me, Rafael, I need to go back."

"See, you're doing it right now."

Well, he's playing with me. I know he's just doing this to distract himself, he's acting like he's attracted to me in some way but please, I'm not the type of girl who attracts guys, my body is not like an hourglass. I am someone who is chubby and I know that this type of body is not very attractive.

"Stop playing with me, let's go back." His expression changed immediately.

"Uh, no, no, no! I didn't mean for you to take it that way, sorry, really!" He says all that with a scared face.

I didn't say anything, I don't know what to say. It's not normal for me that this kind of thing happens, after all, I'm an extra character... right?

Rafale stepped aside and I went back to the room but I felt uncomfortable. It was midnight and we all received our gifts, my mom gave me a super big sweater—I loved it—, my dad gave me money, and my sister a book—this one, yes, she knows me.

I gave my gifts and they opened them, the only ones that were different were those of my parents and my sister, those of the others were the same, except Rafael's, as I did with things from here it looks "personalized."

"Thank you."

Chapter 25

BROOKE

I was looking at the gift box that was on my nightstand. It was her gift but given the circumstances I won't be able to give it to her.

I was at my parent's house, we already received gifts and ate and now we are just enjoying the morning. It is nine o'clock and they—and more other relatives—are in the living room drinking coffee and I think hot chocolate. I should be with them but I'm not in the mood. It bothers me that I couldn't enjoy this day with her and to make the situation worse, my birthday is in January and she won't be able to be there.

Just out of anger, I threw a shirt that was on the bed.

I left the room and without being seen I left the house, nothing is open at this time and well, it's Christmas. I received a white mug with the phrase "the best son."

I'm the only one they have.

After the "incident", there was no more work to do. I think that because of the holidays, the recruiters decided to give the hunt a break. Thiago and I didn't have that much contact afterwards, after the thing in the park we didn't talk anymore. I feel like I'm exaggerating, I shouldn't behave like that.

JASMINE

Well, after living with him, it's not so bad. After the gifts, Rafa apologized a thousand times, he didn't want me to think badly of him and he apologized for how he behaved.

More than half a week has passed, and there are only three days left until it is the new year. Rafa and I managed to be friends, we talked about anything, we were together when we went out to the living room and we both even went to the store.

I have a friend!

I will also say that there were uncomfortable situations between us. One night I couldn't sleep and I went out to get a glass of milk—I was wearing a robe like pajamas, but it was a little short and the fabric wasn't thick, so it could easily see my panties—, I went into the kitchen and I swear I didn't I saw no one and, as normal, I poured myself my milk but I stood there for a few minutes just thinking.

I stretched and my robe went up, I heard an "ehem" and I turned around and there he was. Rafa only had pants, no shirt. I didn't know what to do at that moment, I had forgotten that I was stretching and I looked down and immediately lowered my arms; I ran towards my room.

The next morning I couldn't see his face and that idiot just laughed at me. Afterwards we both laughed at the situation. Right now we were both on the patio drinking coffee, our parents decided to go out to town and our brothers stayed here like us.

"So you haven't graduated from high school yet?"

"No, I was supposed to graduate last year but there was a problem with my subscription and I stayed a year behind."

"You must have missed your friends," I didn't respond immediately. I kept thinking, did I really have friends in middle school? The truth is that no, they were just classmates but not real friends.

"If I'm honest, no, I didn't have those friends to miss them."

"I see." We both stayed silent, it was obvious that this got awkward. "It must have been sad."

"Sometimes I did feel that way but later I realized that it is better to be alone than in bad company." I looked at him and he smiled at me.

We continued talking about other things and eventually we ran out of coffee, we entered the house and went to the kitchen. We were talking but we stayed silent when we saw such a show in the living room.

Rafa shouted, "Get a room!" Scaring the two people on the couch.

My sister was on top of her boyfriend, still dressed, kissing as if it were the end of the world. They separated immediately upon hearing Rafa, in fact, my eyes could not believe what I saw on Vanessa's neck.

"You should cover that up or *te toca chinga*," I said mockingly. She looked at me confused until I pointed it at her neck and she understood, she ran to her room.

"You couldn't wait a minute?" Rafa mockingly asks his brother.

"Shut your mouth. Jasmine, I'm sorry you had to see that," Owen says embarrassed.

"Yes, well, I'll go with Vane."

I went to my sister's room and found her putting makeup on the hickey Owen just gave her. She looked at me in the mirror and laughed, I joined her in laughing and sat on the bed.

"I swear I almost died, I thought you were my parents."

"No, but maybe you have gone to a room to have some privacy."

"You're right but believe me, when your fever rises you can't help it."

"Gross!" I didn't really mean it but let your sister say it, yes, it's embarrassing to hear it.

I stayed there with her until she finished putting on her makeup. We left the room and found our parents in the living room talking, the brothers were also there. The afternoon flew by, we didn't do much except relax.

Rafa's dad bought fireworks and said that there was a place where it is allowed to light these things. For the new year.

It's night and we were outside. I was as comfortable as possible, I had my pajamas that had books as a design, warm socks, a blanket and a cup of hot chocolate, what more could I ask for?

When my sister had mentioned that it would be a shared trip with her boyfriend's family, I thought it was something very quick to do, they have only been dating for months but it turned out well, everyone gets along well.

I finished my drink and got up to go for more. Wrapped in my blanket I walked inside the cabin. I entered and went to the kitchen, about to serve myself, my phone started ringing. Without seeing who it was, I answered.

"Hello?"
"I thought you weren't going to answer me." I stayed silent, processing if it was really the person I was listening to. "I know you didn't expect me to call you but I really miss you *Boneca*."
"I won't talk to you... don't call me again, please."
"Please don't ask me that, anything but that. I know that what you discovered scared you and…"
"That it scared me? Thiago, I wasn't scared, I was terrified." I had that feeling that you don't expect that someone who cares about you can hurt you. "I don't want anything to do with you or Brooke, so please don't contact me again"
"Why haven't you charged us with the police?"
"..."
"If you really don't want anything to do with us, with me, then why haven't you talked to the police?"

Chapter 26

JASMINE

At this point I wanted to cry, why? I don't even know why. How am I supposed to respond to that? Telling him it's because I don't have the courage? Tell him because I don't want him to hurt me? What am I supposed to answer?!

> "Let's just leave it like this, please." I tried with all my might not to shed a tear.
> "No! I want us to be able to fix this, I'm not going to let you go."
> "We are nothing so leave me alone…"

"Jasmine? Are you okay?" I turn around immediately when I hear him. Rafa.

"Yes, everything is fine, don't worry." I tried to smile at him but it was more like a grimace. "Would you give me a second?" He hesitated to leave but in the end he left.

> Thiago asks angrily, "Who was he?" I could notice the sudden change in his voice.
> "You don't mind. Bye and have a good night." I ended the call without letting him answer.

I put the phone aside and let myself fall, I sat on the floor and took long breaths to calm myself down. I had my hands clenched into fists.

Should I feel overwhelmed by this?

I met Thiago for a few weeks, I told him about my problems, he made me feel welcome in his house when I didn't want to return to mine, and we almost... we almost kissed.

When I felt calmer I wrapped myself in my blanket again,—I had dropped it when I was talking to him—and I went towards the back door but Rafa was standing there, I guess he was waiting for me.

"You can talk to me, you know you can." I can but I don't want to, if I talk, I would be exposing them.

"I appreciate that you want to listen to me but it's nothing, don't worry."

"That it was 'nothing'? Woman, you were almost entering an emotional trance, you have a problem and it has to do with whoever you were talking to." I didn't say anything, he's right. "I know we're not the best of soul friends and you know me a few days ago, in fact, if it weren't for this trip we wouldn't have met, not soon at least."

Does it affect me so much that they have been the only friends I have always had? Does it affect me so much that they are no longer with me? Do I feel so lonely?

I didn't answer him and he understood, we both went out and sat together on one of the sofas, Vanessa and I looked at each other and she noticed that I wasn't okay but she didn't say anything. Everyone was happy, drinking and eating snacks. My sister was snuggling with Owen and they looked very comfortable. Rafa had his arm around me, hugging me and it felt good, it felt good to be in this position.

"Well, we'll go to the cabin, don't stay so late and behave guys," says Rafa's mother as she stops with her husband.

"Us too, tomorrow we have to prepare things for the new year," my mom says now.

"But it's still the 28th," I look at the time on my phone. "Well 29th."

"*Entre mas pronto, mejor.*" They say finally and leave.

Only the four of us stayed outside, around the campfire. The night is quiet and the atmosphere soft. I would like to stay like this forever. I really would like that but things don't last forever.

I can't sleep. I want to sleep but I can't.

I look at the time on my phone for the fifth time, 4:27 AM.

I don't want to go back to having to eat the gummies to sleep. When I was a little girl, I had a lot of trouble sleeping. My mom was worried and took me to the doctor but they couldn't find anything. They just told her to give me the gummies every once in a while and eventually I was able to sleep well and stopped eating them.

I don't like to stay up late because I just spend all my time thinking about nonsense, well not always but it depends on how I'm feeling. I thought about the boys, what would have happened if I had never seen that message, would they have told me at some point? They didn't do anything to me after I discovered them and that was something.

Are they waiting for me to make a move? They wait for me to go to the police?

I try to sleep, I don't want to wake up with dark circles under my eyes—although I doubt it.

I looked at the sun coming out of the window, it should be something nice to see but seeing it means that I really didn't sleep at all. I have no choice but to get up and get ready for the day. I went to the bathroom and took a bath; I changed into black leggings and a dark green long-sleeved shirt.

I left the room and went to the kitchen, I made myself a bowl of cereal and sat at the table, while I ate I watched videos on my phone.

Half an hour later, I see Rafa's mother leave her room and without noticing me, she approaches the coffee pot and prepares her own cup. She turns around and when she sees me she lets out a scream.

"My God," she says and she puts her hand on her chest. "Jasmine, I didn't know you were there." I just smiled at her.

Minutes later the others came out with confused faces, they asked what that scream was and the lady explained to them, they laughed a little and then they had breakfast. Rafa sat next to me and stared at me.

"A photo lasts longer." My comment makes him laugh

"Would you give me a photo of yourself?"

"On second thought, no."

"At least I tried," he got up again and went for coffee and returned to the same place. "Have you eaten yet?" I nodded.

"Only cereal…"

"Didn't you sleep well? Your eyes look red."

Chapter 27

THIAGO

Fuck. Fuck. Fuck!

I was debating with myself whether to go to where she is or wait for her to return.

I felt happy to hear her voice after so long, I really missed her, but how is it possible that she is with a boy? Isn't she supposed to have gone on a trip with her family? She has no male brothers!

I didn't know what to do, I wanted to go to her but I knew she would be more upset with me, so that is not an option. I didn't want to just stay here doing nothing, but what else could I do?

I put my hands on my head and pulled my hair because I was so frustrated. After all...

We are nothing.

I must admit that it did hurt me when she said that but I still have hope, if she hasn't reported us to the police yet, it means that there is still a chance to get closer to her. Right now I am on the porch of my house, I am sitting on the steps watching people walk by, some people avoid passing by and cross over to the other sidewalk.

It's midday and I don't know what to do. In my head there is only her, her voice, her face, and her body, that body that drives me crazy, those thick legs, her hips, even that waist that can be noticed with every step.

I felt my pants tighten and I knew it was time to stop thinking about her body. I went inside the house and went straight to the bathroom and took care of my problem.

It's already night and I'm walking to the store. I will only buy a few things, the truth is that I go more often because it reminds me of her. The first time we spoke. I entered and went straight to where the drinks were, I grabbed some sodas but I was tempted to buy beer.

In the end I bought a box. I returned to my house and entered, it is calmer now that those who fathered me are no longer here. I stayed in the living room and turned on the TV, there wasn't much so I turned on the news. They were announcing that they caught a hitman, he was in the middle of an assassination attempt when they caught him.

They are always smarter than others and that one does not fit into that category.

I laughed a little and drank my beer, it would seem like I'm relaxing but I'm not; I want my *Boneca* to be by my side, to be with me. I have to find out who that bastard who was with her is, how long he has known her and where he lives, so I can give him a visit.

"Jasmine, you're okay, my ass." I finished the bitter liquid and grabbed another can.

I continued drinking until I left the box half empty, —it was a box of twelve cans—after all I am the son of some drunk duds but I am smarter.

I fell asleep on the couch. I woke up at eight in the morning but I didn't feel like doing anything. My head hurt so I went to the kitchen and grabbed some pills, I poured myself a glass of water and then I went to take a shower.

I left the bathroom and sat in the chair, turned on the monitors and checked the messages, there were none.

They also celebrate holidays.

I had a gift for her. It was a large lilac sweater, she has several in her closet and I know she doesn't have one of this color. The sweater has a small rose on one of the sleeves, it's small but it looks good. It looks good on her. I didn't know whether to give it to her or not, I was afraid she would reject it.

I finished dressing and dried my hair, it has been growing and I haven't cut it, it is below my shoulders. I brushed it and made it into a half tail, so it doesn't get in the way of my face.

It's December 30th, and there's only one day left until the new year. I wonder what she is doing, if she already woke up, if she already ate, what is she doing? I would like to send someone to her but, first, I don't know where she is, second, I don't have so many resources to do it, yes, I have money but I wouldn't dare to do this to her; she has enough with this.

I hear my door knock, I go down to the living room and open the door, it's Brooke with a worried expression, which I didn't like at all.

"What's happening?" He came in, I closed the door and looked at him. "Well?"

"Mindy plans to ambush her on the first day of school." He didn't need to say a name, I already knew who he was talking about.

"What? What are you talking about?"

"Today I saw her at the cafe next to the park. She was there meeting with some dudes and girls, they were talking about what to do about Jasmine."

I couldn't believe what he was saying, this was getting out of control and all for attention? This is too much. I looked at Brooke and he saw that I was tense. I hate that they touch what is mine and whoever touches them suffers the consequences.

"Give me the address of that stupid girl."

"What are you going to do?" I stopped looking at him, I looked at the ground.

"I will only talk to her, I am not a scoundrel to hit a woman." I said that but I know that if she dares to do something, I will not see her as a woman, I will see her as just another scum of this world.

Brooke left, leaving me alone, he gave me the address but he said he didn't want to be part of this, that he would help Jasmine in another way. I did not care. If this girl wants attention, then I will give her attention.

I went to the basement and grabbed a small blade and some special gloves so it wouldn't slip. It's early but it doesn't matter. On holidays is when more "accidents" happen.

Chapter 28

JASMINE

I already had my things packed, I only had two changes of clothes and a pair of pajamas outside. There is only tomorrow until the new year and I am excited, I knew the wishes to ask for; Vanessa already took care of buying the twelve grapes.

I was eating fruit salad that my mom had made, I was eating with my sister and Rafa, Owen was helping his dad make who knows what.

"What should we do right now? I want to do something before we go back to LA," I said while looking at my spoon with fruit.

My sister asks, "Like what?"

"I don't know, maybe go to town or walk down the street, from my window I could see that the road is long and there were lights, I guess from other cabins."

"Sounds good, let me ask my *ma'* to see what she says." Vanessa gets up and goes to look for my mom.

"The salad is good, you should give me the recipe so I can make it myself."

"It's not that difficult to do but everyone has their own touch to give." He nods and focuses all his attention on his plate, he looks like a little child trying sugar for the first time.

A while later I was changing, my mom had said that we could go out. As expected, only the boys and us were going out.

Why do adults always do things between adults? Vanessa and Owen are already adults, but they don't take care of their "attendance", what about me? Well, I'm the baby.

I dressed in leggings, tennis shoes and one of the shirts I had bought. I left the room and met the others.

"Ready," I said and they saw me.

"Okay, let's go then," says Owen, giving me a hat, it was starting to get sunny. It was still cold but the sun was at full brightness.

We left the cabin and started walking, and I was right, there were more cabins and they looked pretty, some were bigger than others as well as some smaller than others. As far as I know, most of the cabins are rented but there are some where people do live in them.

The pine trees were very tall, there was snow resting on the branches and small drops of water were falling.

"The landscape looks nice," says Rafa, standing next to me.

"Yeah. I wish I could live in a place like this."

He asked randomly, "Nice shirt, was it your dad's?"

"What? No, I bought it in one of the stores in town." I said, confused.

"Oh, okay." He smiles nervously and with some relief, as if he was expecting another answer but I ignored that and continued looking at the place.

We reached the end of the street because there were no more cabins and there was no more path. We returned and then went to the town, everyone went their own way, so I went to see the wood crafts. They had necklaces with little dolls made of wood, all of different figurines.

I approached the rack where the necklaces were hanging. There were flowers and animals, but one that had a small rose caught my attention, it was painted and I was surprised by the details. I asked for the price and bought it. I won't see a necklace like that anywhere else again so I grabbed it.

Happy I left the store and put on the necklace; nothing could be more beautiful.

When I left the store, I went to look for the others. After a while, I found my sister looking at some dresses inside a small store, so I walked in and approached her.

"What are you doing?"

"This dress is pretty, *eda*?" She lifts up a dress that possibly reaches above her knees, it has straps and is forest green with simple white embroidery.

"Yes it's pretty."

She buys the dress and we both leave the store. We continued walking for a while longer and then we decided that it was time to return. My sister called her boyfriend—Rafa was already with him—to tell him that we were going to return to the cabin. Along the way, she looked at some flowers and even saw some little squirrels.

When we arrived, my dad was coming out of the cabin, before we asked he said he was going to the store. We just said "ok" and walked in.

I was making my bed when Vanessa entered my room in a hurry. I looked at her confused, she came in and closed the door and turned around looking at me with an expression of excitement and amazement at the same time.

"What's happening? Why do you come like this?"

"Owen gave me a promise ring."

"A what?"

"A promise ring, do you know what that means?" I didn't understand what she was referring to but I remembered what those rings meant.

"*No!*"

"*Si!*"

I didn't know how to respond to that. A promise ring? So soon? The two of them have only been dating for two to three months!

"Vanessa, you haven't been dating for even a year, you haven't finished university, you don't have a stable job, you..."

Interrupting me she says, "There is still time for all that, what has to be done will still be done."

The truth is that I did not expect that, perhaps for many people it is not a big deal but, for us, a promise like that is something big and real. If the relationship fails—I hope not—that would break my sister. I hope that they can truly become happy and that they both achieve their goals.

After the news, we talked a little more about other things and then she went to her room, of course, not before telling me not to say anything to my mom because she still doesn't know. I stayed in my room watching a movie on my phone. I only got halfway through it because I was already feeling tired.

I went to the bathroom and took a shower. When I left I changed into pajama pants, brushed my hair and dried myself a little with the towel.

Only tomorrow and I return home, after a few days I return to school and there are possibilities of seeing them.

I know I was entertained throughout the trip and I had fun but after having that call, I just thought about many things and mostly about them. I couldn't sleep the night before and I know that tonight will be the same. Yes, I'm tired but I don't think I can sleep.

I made my bed and made myself as comfortable as possible and went to bed.

9:30 PM

...

10:15 PM

...

11:53 PM

...

03:19 AM

...

I thought so.

Chapter 29

JASMINE

We were all in *chinga*. By coincidence, no one set the alarm because they thought someone else had set it. There were only two bathrooms and they were occupied and we were all rushing others.

I, on the other hand, was already bathed and changed,—since I didn't sleep all night, I got ready ahead of time—I was waiting for them to make something to eat. I would have done something but my mom clearly told me "Don't do anything because we are going to make breakfast."

I'm hungry.

My mom finished getting ready and went straight to the kitchen. I don't know what the others were doing, I saw that they were carrying bags and backpacks and I don't know what other things, tomorrow is the first of January and New Year's and we are supposed to go to the space to light artificial fires. What was the rush? No idea.

"*Mija, tu ya estas?*" my dad asks me while he adjusts his belt.

"*Sipi.*"

"*Bueno,*" he says and goes to the room.

My mom puts me a plate with some eggs, sausage, and warm tortillas. I, happily, begin to eat; my sister and the others come over to eat and when they finish the parents sit down to eat. Today I woke up cold and I dressed in jeans, a simple black shirt and the sweater that my mom gave me for Christmas.

"Jasmine, are you sleeping?" my sister asks me.

"Yeah why?" What a liar I am.

"These last two days I have seen you more tired than normal and with your eyes a little red."

"Okay, not so much, I do try, but I end up watching videos or I just stare at the ceiling more than normal."

She asks worriedly, "Have you told my mom?"

"I don't want to worry her, and I bet she'll give me the gummies again and I don't want to, those things make me feel like I'm on drugs, and make me feel sick.

Well, basically that's the job of gummies, they drug you to make you sleep.

In the end they told us that today we were supposed to leave, I don't know where but we had to go because we were already getting late. It's ten o'clock AM.

We got in the truck and the others in their car, I noticed that we left the town and the road was only trees and more flora. My eyes felt heavy and I really wanted to sleep but the position I was in didn't help much. I turned around and saw Vaessa, I was tempted to lie down on her, she saw me and understood what I wanted to do, she took her hands off of her lap and I put my head on her lap.

I relaxed so much that I fell asleep.

After what felt like twenty minutes I woke up and noticed that we were just stopping in another town. I stood up straight and stretched, my body felt so good.

I finally got some sleep, two nights in a row is not a good thing.

"How much sleep did I get?" I asked Vanessa.

"The whole trip." She smiles at me as if it were a good thing.

"And how long was the trip? It felt like twenty minutes or more."

"Twenty minutes? It was a trip of almost three hours." I looked at her in disbelief, was it really three hours? "I know you don't believe it but it's true and I'm glad you were able to sleep."

"Yeah."

We got off the truck and we all went into the place. It was a very colorful place, there were many stalls and many people, apparently the place is very popular. We were in a group, I was in the middle of my mom and my dad, and Vanessa was already like gum with Owen. The others were on our side as was Rafa, he saw me and smiled at me, I smiled at him too and continued looking at the place.

We hardly go out but when we do we make sure to go somewhere where we can all enjoy ourselves. My mom and I separated and went to a stand where they sold homemade popsicles. It was cold but it never hurts to eat something cold. She bought it for everyone and we returned to the group. I grabbed a strawberry and kiwi one.

The day was exhausting. After looking around, we went to a restaurant to eat. I wouldn't give the place five stars but the food was at least passable. When we finished eating I looked for the place on my phone and as I expected, it also had negative comments about the place.

Next time I'll look at the reviews before going somewhere to eat.

We returned to the cabin and finished picking up and cleaning. Everyone made sure they had their things ready and then we loaded them into the truck, it's already after five and we were getting ready to leave, well, after we went to do the fireworks and wait for twelve .

Rafa calls me, "Jasmine, come see this."

"What?"

"Come on, you'll like it." I looked at him confused but I followed him.

We went to the back of the cabin and I couldn't believe what my eyes were seeing. It was a deer that was giving birth, it was retired and could easily be covered by the trees and bushes but we could see well.

She was lying on the ground and at times she raised her head, she had half her body already out, minutes later she expelled everything, the deer got up and approached her fawn, she moved it with her nose and it responded.

I said in a whisper, "How beautiful…" I know she couldn't hear me but I felt like I could ruin such a beautiful moment.

"When I looked at her, I thought she was hurt but I noticed her big belly and she lay down and I knew that she really wasn't hurt."

"I have never seen anything like this." I keep seeing the new mother, I see how she starts to walk and her baby goes behind her. "I hope her path is safe."

"Don't worry, it will."

We returned to the truck and I immediately went to tell my sister. While we were talking they told us that it was time and we got into the truck. My dad started the engine and started the trip, again.

I like going out but sitting for so many hours I don't like it very much.

I don't do many activities but when I sit for a long time, my legs get stiff and sometimes they give me cramps and well, that's not good at all.

Once again I tried to sleep but I couldn't, I didn't feel tired, not much at least.

Chapter 30

BROOKE

I can't believe it's time to go back to school but the fact that I'm changing to go to school makes it even more believable. I'm excited but I'm still nervous. I want to try to talk to her again but I don't know if she'll allow me.

I button the last button on my shirt and take the non-existent dust off my pants. I look at myself one last time in the mirror and leave my room with my things. I go down the stairs and grab the keys.

I get in my car and start driving, I live nearby but I have other things to do after school. It's January and the heat is just beginning to be felt. It looks like a nice day and I hope it continues that way and ends.

I got to school and parked, grabbed my backpack and got out of the car. I stared at the building for a moment, I really hope I can talk to her or at least see that she is okay. I passed through the main door and went to my respective classroom. I only shared a class with her and if I'm lucky, I will see her at lunch.

True, she doesn't eat here. Well, I'll have a way to see her.

I entered my classroom and saw several people half asleep in their seats and others greeting others. There were still a few minutes before classes started so I left my things in my seat and went to the cafeteria. I'll see what there is for breakfast.

I entered the place and there were several people, more than I thought. There were small groups giving gifts and others crowding around wishing each other a Merry Christmas and a Happy New Year.

I want to do that...

I got in line and while I was waiting I started looking at things on my phone but I was interrupted, felt a tap on my shoulder and I turned to see who it was.

"Hello!" And we got off to a bad start. I gave her a nod and continued with my things but I think she had other plans. "Merry Christmas and Happy New Year! Look, I even bring you a gift," she says and lifts up a bag with Rudolf smiling.

"Uhm, thank you?" I didn't want to receive anything from her.

After Thiago went to "visit" her, I didn't want to see how she was doing, I didn't really care, I just wanted her not to do anything to Jasy. I took the bag hoping she would leave. She smiles satisfied and I see that she is looking at something behind me, confused, I turned around and saw her.

No...

I turn around immediately and see that Mindy is gone. What just happened? I tried to see Jasmine again but she was gone, too. Did she just use me?

Brooke, damn it, you're smarter than this, there's no way this just happened!

The bell rang indicating the start of classes. I refrained from going to look for her, I went to my classes and I had no choice but to wait to meet her. I arrived at the classroom and sat down reluctantly, just when the day was beginning calmly.

Just as I expected. Yes I was able to see Jasy on several occasions but she always ignored me, Mindy no longer bothered me afterward but I know that what she did was part of her plan. I only had one chance left and this time I wouldn't mind making her listen to me.

It's time for the last class and it's the one I share with her. She was sitting in her usual place, there were still a few minutes left so there weren't that many students in the room. I approached her, she didn't look at me, she had her gaze on her phone but I saw that she wasn't doing anything.

"Jasy?" I said in a low voice, but she didn't respond. "I know that maybe you don't want to see me, much less talk to me, but I really would like you to listen to me."

There was no movement on her part for a few minutes and when I thought she would say something, the bell rang and they began to enter the classroom. I was going to return to my seat but Jasy spoke.

"After class…" I smiled as much as I could, I was finally able to listen to her after so long.

I just said "okay" and went back to my seat. I know, no, I'm *confident* that for sure after this we can continue as before. The class went normally, we didn't do much because the teacher didn't even want to be here.

I noticed that Jasy left first, I didn't want to go right away, I didn't want her to see that I'm desperate,—although yes, I am, anyway, that's not the case—I gathered my things and slowly left the school.

First, I looked for her in front of the school but she wasn't there and then I remembered that what we were going to talk about was not something that should not be done publicly so I went towards the back. There she was, sitting on the bench looking everywhere. She is nervous. I went to where she is and stood facing her, she saw me and stood up straight in her seat.

After a few seconds I spoke, "Hi Jasy, how are you?"

"I'm fine but we're not here to talk about how we are," she says, being direct, which surprised me a little.

"Yes you're right. I suppose you have a lot of questions in mind and I know you want me to answer them but before I take all this further I would like to ask you just one, well two questions." She looked at me in doubt but nodded. "Do you think that, after what we talk, you will come back to stop talking to me? And the other question is, why didn't you go to the police?"

Jasmine looked at me for a few minutes without saying anything, I really wanted to know what she thought. She became a special person for me. In that short time we shared it was enough to know the type of person she is and they are one of those people that you would like to have around.

"For your first question, I'm not sure, it all depends on what we can talk about and your second question... I wouldn't know how to answer you..."

"Okay, let's talk then."

Jasmine is showing a somewhat nervous and defensive body language. I know that her trust in me is low but I am really willing to earn her trust again. Besides, if I can make her happy with me, I will be able to be close to her so I can protect her from the crazy woman.

Chapter 31

JASMINE

I agreed to talk to him but I was already regretting it. I am not good at confrontations and this is not just any confrontation. Will this be the same after speaking? How am I supposed to do that? Brooke looked happy when I agreed to talk to him.

How can a boy as sweet as him do such a thing?

I was waiting for him to speak, I wasn't going to start this conversation. He was still standing and he didn't seem to want to sit down so he was just waiting.

"There is no excuse for what you saw and I can't tell you that what you saw is a lie," he began to say. "But I also want you to know that I am not capable of hurting you, even if I do what I do, I would never do anything to you."

"Why do you do it?" was the first thing I asked.

"It's like a job, they pay us to do things and I do it for the money and I think... for fun... I guess."

"Fun?" I said without believing. "Do you murder for fun?"

"It's not something I do often! What is mainly my job is to hack systems on computers, cell phones and things like that," he says quickly.

"Do you realize what you are telling me? Do you do that for fun, yes, that thing about computers, knowing codes can be entertaining but, Brooke, hacking others stuff for fun?" I couldn't process everything he was telling me. "Do you also do it for money? You do know that there are other jobs, right? Your skills can attract a very good job and you can get good money out of it."

"I know it sounds ugly but... the truth is that I can't explain it to you, I don't have the right words," he says, already a little scared.

"Why did you decide to talk to me in the first place?" It was something I really wanted to know from the first moment he sat at the table in the cafeteria. Brooke looked at me with confusion.

"What are you talking about?"

"Brooke, I'm nobody, I'm a girl who watches her adolescence go by as if it were nothing. I don't go out to parties; I have days and nights free. My hobbies are reading and watching movies at home alone or I just spend my time studying but I'm not the best in the class! When I graduate from high school I will probably work in a place where I wrap hamburgers." I said feeling trapped. "I do not have friends! When someone approaches me, it doesn't last even a month and they leave. *You*, why did you decide to talk to me?" I was out of breath. Brooke stared at me and I could see how his eyes turned red.

We were both silent. Neither of us said anything. At this point I was already crying. I really love Brooke, I really do, I would like to continue being his friend but things like this don't happen in real life. In a book it would be something exciting, but, in what book is the protagonist innocent of doing something? In what book does the protagonist not think about everything else, about her family?

But I'm not the protagonist! I am the daughter of immigrants who came to the United States to have a better life, of parents who want the best for their daughters. The American dream!

Being friends with him, him and Thiago would be hiding things that I know my mentality could not sustain for long and I know that at some point I would ruin it, whose fault would it be? Well mine.

What the hell do they want from me?

"I... I just want my little Jasy back..." he says with a broken voice.

Tears fell from my eyes, from the beginning Brooke acted like a brother to me and he always made it clear to me with his actions. He was the brother I never had.

"You asked me why I hadn't gone to the police, well, because I didn't want to take the blame for putting you two in that horrible place. I didn't want to be thinking, for all my life, that it was me who put you there." My breathing was fast, I felt a lump in my throat but I had to talk to him.

"You know I wouldn't let you feel like that."

"But I would! I am a person who thinks too much, thousands of things happen in this small head, it would be impossible for me not to think about it, it would be impossible not to feel guilt. Do you think I don't want to be friends? Keep going out talking at breakfast, go to the mall and buy a milkshake? I wish for those outings as you can't imagine, because you were the first and only friend I had."

I said what I had to say, my hands were already clenched into fists and I didn't know what else to do. I want to hear what he has to say but he doesn't say anything. I notice how he tightens his grip on his backpack.

"I do not know what to tell you..."

"The thing is, there's nothing more to say Brooke..." At this time there was no one at school, a lot of time had already passed and I hadn't realized that it was getting late.

Do we last that long?

"Jasy..."

"Jasmine?" Someone said my name and we turned to see who it was. "Is everything okay?"

Rafa.

"Yes, yes, everything is fine." I quickly wiped my tears and with a little paper that I had I wiped my nose.

"I went to your house but your mom told me that you hadn't arrived yet," he says and then looks at Brooke. "Hi. Rafael." He extends his hand but Brooke doesn't accept it. "Okay."

"Yes, well, I got a little distracted." I wanted to smile but it didn't turn out well.

"Are you sure you're okay, your eyes are red, were you crying?" Rafa was going to get closer to me but Brooke stopped him by standing in front of me.

"Brooke, please stop. Come on, I finished what I was doing here." And I left. I know that Rafa had doubts but he knew that I was not going to answer him. I wanted to look back but cowardice wouldn't let me, I knew that if I looked at him I would start crying again.

We arrived at the house and with a silent apology I went to my room, I couldn't hold it back anymore and I started to cry. There was so much feeling that I had trapped in my chest that I let go of everything, I grabbed my pillow and hugged it tightly.

I heard the door open and then some arms surrounded me. I knew it was my sister because of the smell of perfume that she always wears. I cried even harder.

"Shhh, everything will be okay."

"No, it won't be…"

Chapter 32

THIAGO

I feel uneasy. There is something about this day that doesn't leave me alone. Today I woke up fine but something felt out of place. I looked at the time on my phone, it's already after three.

My Boneca already left school.

I was tempted to go but I held back and in the end I didn't go, I don't think she wants to see me yet. I made myself a sandwich and went to the living room to eat it. I looked out the window at some people from school. Minutes passed and I didn't see her.

Maybe she stayed doing some chores.

I waited even longer and half an hour had passed, and still there was no sign of her. I got up from the couch and just when I was going to open the door, I looked at her along with someone else, a guy.

Who the hell is that piece of shit? How the hell does she know that man?

I stared at the two of them until I lost sight of them. I stood there like an idiot looking at the window, I still didn't assimilate what I saw; not having friends is not knowing anyone, right? I grabbed the phone and immediately called Brooke, they were coming from school so maybe he could have seen something or knew something. On the third ring he answered.

> "Who the hell is that who came with Jasmine?"
> "..." he didn't respond, but I could hear his breathing.
> "Answer me! Who was that?"
> "She...she doesn't like me anymore...she doesn't even want to see me..."
> "What are you talking about?" I heard him let out a sigh.
> "Today I asked her to talk and..."

I let Brooke tell me everything that happened today, he told me what she told him, how she felt and when that guy arrived. I didn't know she felt that way, I couldn't know. I want to go to her and hug her but from what Brooke tells me, she's not okay.

> "You would have seen her face, it was broken, full of sadness and I caused that." At this point he was already in tears, normally I would say that crying is nonsense but given the situation, it is not the time to say something like that.
> "Go rest, let's let things calm down and we'll see what to do." I said and then ended the call.

Merda...

I waited for it to get dark, I really wanted to go see her, make sure she was okay. It being ten o'clock at night, I changed into pants and a long sleeve shirt, both black. I left my house and through the back of it I went to hers. There were some lights on, I guess her parents are still awake.

I got to where her window is and I saw her, there she was. Jasmine was lying on her bed hugging her pillow, she was wearing her pajamas and had her hair down.

She had a tired look. I couldn't see her in more detail because she didn't have her light on, she only had a lamp. The door opened and her sister came in, she sat on the edge of the bed and put her hand on Jasmine's hip. She spoke to her but she didn't move.

I wish I could hear what she says.

Three hours have passed and she still hasn't fallen asleep. After eleven o'clock struck I settled on the floor so I wouldn't be standing all the time and so I could continue watching her. I was hoping she would fall asleep so I could go into her room but she just won't sleep; her sister left after talking to her and she just stayed in the same position.

She's really having a hard time. I feel like this is all my fault and Brooke was right, I just invaded her peace of mind and now she is like this because of the same thing.

A few minutes passed and she was still the same. I decided that it was time to go so I got up and looked at her one last time. About to leave I looked at how she brought her hands to her face, her body began to have little spasms... she is crying.

I felt my chest squeeze. I stopped looking at her and stared at the grass, I couldn't see her crying, I couldn't stand seeing her that way. I have to go, if I don't I'll want to go in and hug her and I know that's not what she wants right now.

I said I would get rid of the shit that walks in this place but apparently I am that shit.

I started walking and went home. When I arrived I went straight to my room, took a shower and when I came out I turned on the monitor. After the "visit" I gave that crazy woman, I made sure to install a small camera so I could keep an eye on her. I looked at the screen and there she was, she was lying on her bed looking at her phone.

She got up and took something out from under her bed, it was a shoe box, she opened it and took out a small bag with something white inside it. I looked with confusion at what I was seeing, she had the look that she was about to do something and something not very good.

"If that's what I'm thinking, I hope and don't do something stupid with it."

Mindy put the bag in her backpack and then went to sleep. I really wanted to think that she wouldn't do something so stupid, I told her myself that if she tried to do something to Jasmine, she would see me again and not just to talk.

I turned off the monitor and went to bed. I really didn't want anything bad to happen, I just wanted Jasmine to have a normal day tomorrow. With Jasmine's smile being my last thought I fell asleep.

I woke up agitated. I had sweat on my forehead and was breathing hard. I had a nightmare, it should have been a dream because I dreamed of her but we were not in a good situation.

It was a dream, dreams don't come true, it's all in my mind...

I really wanted what I heard to be buried deep in my mind.

Chapter 33

JASMINE

It's been a few days since I left Brooke standing on that school bench. They were blue days, I didn't feel like doing anything, I just did the same thing every day, I got up, got ready, went to school, came back and did my homework, ate, took a bath and went to sleep. The same routine without change.

Rafa came to the house a few times, I knew that he was asking about me but I didn't want him to see me in this state, but the messages that he sent me I did answer them.

My sister was in charge of coming to my room these days to ask me how I was doing, I just answered that I was fine. But the truth is that I didn't know how I felt, was I really that depressed about this? Part of me felt ridiculous.

"*Mija*, Rafa came," my mom says. Every time he comes, my mom came and told me

"It's okay." I think today I feel a little better, I had to calm down and continue as if nothing happened.

I'll ignore what I know about the two of them. I will ignore that I met them at some point. I will ignore that we were friends.

I left the room and found him eating a quesadilla that my mom gave him.

"Hi." Rafa sees me and smiles.

"Hi, how are you?"

"I'm better than other days."

"Glad to hear it. I came because I wanted to know if you want to go for a little trip." I didn't expect that question, I really didn't but, as I said before, I have to continue, besides, Rafa is also my friend

"Sure, just let me change, I'm not going to go out with this," I said while pointing to myself.

I had gray pants and a black hoodie, I had my hair done in a braid but it was messy. I went to my room and changed into black jeans, a large dark blue long-sleeved shirt, and some tennis shoes. I brushed my hair and now it was more presentable. I left the room and saw that Vanessa was talking to Rafa.

"Thank you," she says in a whisper, Rafa smiles at her and then he sees me.

"Ready?" I just nod. "Okay, let's go."

We left the house and got into his car,zfI just found out that he had a car. I looked at it during one of his visits—he started it and started driving.

We passed by the corner store, through the park and continued until we reached the street where all kinds of people set up their small stalls and started selling; I have rarely come here but from what I have seen they have many nice things.

"Let's go," says Rafa, getting out of the car, I took off my seat belt and got out anyway.

We entered and the first thing I saw was the crowd of people, a child could easily get lost in a place like this. We both entered and looked at each stall we passed. We talked a little during the course, I asked him about his day and what he's been doing, he asked me the same thing but unlike him, I haven't done much.

We stopped at a bracelet stand, even there the lady was making more. Some were just thread and others had pebbles.

"Since the other day I wanted to come here but I didn't want to come alone, so today I tried to see if I could get you out."

"And you did."

"Yeah."

While he was looking at the bracelets, I looked around, there were also stalls selling jewelry, shoes, clothes and even food. I felt him take my hand and I turned around, Rafa was putting a bracelet on my wrist.

I asked, confused, "And this?"

"It's a small gift, I remember that when we were in New Mexico you said that you would like to share these kinds of things with a friend, so here I am." I looked at his wrist and like me, he had a bracelet but the difference was that mine had an "R" and his had a "J".

"I'm surprised that you remember." I felt happy.

"We can do all those things you want to do, even just be at home watching a movie." I looked at him and he had a smile on his face, he looked at me and I gave off emotion, excitement for what he was doing.

"Can we really do all this?" He nods. "I could be a bother."

"I don't mind."

"There are many things I want to do."

"Even better."

"What if I want to put a mask on you?"

"I'm all yours."

I couldn't hold back the emotion and I rushed towards him and hugged him. He will let me do all the things I want.

The rest of the day we spent on this street looking at the other stalls. We stopped to eat and talked a little, well more so because I had no topic of conversation.

He took me back to the house and when I entered my sister was on the couch on her phone. When she saw me, she smiled from ear to ear, got up and approached me. Vanessa took me by the arm and took me to her room.

"Well?"

"Well what?"

"How was your outing with my brother-in-law, what did you do? Where did you go?"

"Well, we went to the market street, and he bought me this bracelet." I raised my hand and showed it to her. "He also bought one."

"How pretty! And you say that he also bought one?" I nod. "*Miralo.*"

"It felt good, you know. I finally have a friend with whom I can talk, do things and share moments."

"Jasmine, you do know that, sometimes, friends become something else," she says, getting a little serious.

"I'm not eleven years old, I know what you're talking about but... don't you think that telling me this now would be something uncomfortable, I'm just trying to solve my problems."

"Your problems?"

"Vane, I never had friends, the other two... I just want to have something real. I felt very lonely when I was in middle school, it's the same with high school, what do I have? I have no idea, and I know you've noticed it, but I stopped sleeping."

"Yes, I just didn't want to say anything because I wasn't totally sure."

"I don't want my mom to worry, I don't want them to take me to the hospital, I hate that place."

"Well, let's go back to the beautiful. I just want you to keep in mind that some things can change, you never know when feelings change."

"Yes, I understand."

We talked a little more and then I went to my room. I know Vanessa is right but I've just begun to clear my head and I want to continue that way until I can finally sleep. I know that everything I have in my head doesn't let me sleep and it's a pain in the ass.

I remember that one time I went to therapy to see what I had, to see if it was mental that prevented me from sleeping, it turned out that it was because of stress from school because I didn't have good grades and I felt alone and I didn't talk about my problems with no one and that made me stop sleeping.

It felt a little ridiculous but after a few weeks of therapy, I was able to sleep, I gradually recovered my sleeping hours and continued as a normal person. I don't want to go back to therapy, or to gummies, I just want to continue as someone extra in a story.

Chapter 34

JASMINE

We are in the month of lovers, many at school began to make plans for the fourteenth, the local cinemas will give a discount to couples, the restaurants will have specials and the mall will have merchandise on sale. Even my sister has that day scheduled.

Some classrooms have decorations on their doors and inside, the student committee is making deliveries from student to student. Each year is something different, the first year I was here they gave chocolate strawberries, the second year they were heart-shaped balloons, the third year they were more creative and gave surprise boxes,—that was my favorite, the committee asked for photos and things that the other person liked and they were in charge of sending it—this year they are roses. You ordered roses of the color you wanted and how many and then they sent them.

Right now I'm heading to the cafeteria, I didn't know whether to go get my food or not eat today, anyway I wasn't that hungry.

I approached where they were giving the food and I saw that they were giving heart-shaped cupcakes so I stood in line and grabbed only the pizza and a juice, took my cupcake and threw away the rest.

Right now my mom would tell me something like "you are throwing away the food and the children in Africa with nothing to eat."

I sat at a table alone and took out my computer to do my homework. It's due on Friday but it was better to do it early and then not do anything afterwards, just turn it in. While I was completing the questionnaire I noticed Mindy approaching me, the first thing I did was grab my backpack and put it on my lap.

I know I sound paranoid but I really saw her this morning trying to put something in my backpack and knowing her I know it's not a love letter.

"Hi!" She says with her "best" face in the world.

"Hi…"

"Can I accompany you?" she says, sitting in the chair opposite.

"You are already sitting."

"How are you?" She ignores what I said and claps both hands, she is acting strange and I don't want to find out why.

"Good. Do you need something?"

"Now that you ask, yes, someone asked me on a date and wanted some advice from you."

"An advice? From me?" It is more than clear that she is doing something, a joke perhaps.

"Yup, it's just…" she approaches. "It's about Brooke." She says in a whisper.

She pulls back and looks me in the eyes with a serious look, did he really ask her out? Well, I saw how she gave him a Christmas gift and he accepted it, but did he ask her out? I don't know why I care, I shouldn't care, I decided I had to keep going.

"But what do you need from me? Can't you go talk to someone else?"

"I would like that but given the fact that you two are friends I thought that you could help me."

"He…he and I are not friends." She looks at me with surprise but of course I can see that she is pretending, I always knew when she was lying and when she was telling the truth and right now her attitude makes me look at the farce.

Maybe she is also lying about meeting him...

"Really?! What a surprise, but I still wanted to know what things he likes." I was going to answer something but from behind her I looked at Brooke who was looking this way.

"Why don't you ask him? He's behind you." She turns around and it's my chance to get out of here.

I left the cafeteria and went to the classroom for my next class. When I entered I saw that some students were asleep.

Class started after twenty minutes, it was normal but there was a knock on the door and when the teacher opened it, the committee members entered; They brought many bouquets in hand and began to distribute them. There were yellow, red and pink roses.

I continued with my things because I knew there was nothing for me, that's what the previous three years were like, what difference will there be this time?

"Jasmine Santos?" I raised my head when I heard my name, did I listen well? ""Is Jasmine Santos here?" They did say my name.

I raised my hand and they gave me a bouquet of red roses. I was confused, what is this? I looked for the note and when I found it I opened it immediately.

> "Did you know that not only couples celebrate, but also friends?"
>
> -B

I couldn't believe it, did he really just send me a bouquet? The roses looked beautiful and smelled so good. I smiled a little, I really try to forget "the thing" but how am I supposed to forget it if he does this?

The class ended and then I went to the last class. Yes, I was happy for the bouquet, no one had given me a bouquet before and I felt like a child who had just been given a popsicle. When I entered my class, I looked at him, he was lying on the table with his hands around his head.

Should I say thank you? But I don't want to wake him up.

I went to sit in my chair. The teacher arrived and class began. From time to time I looked towards where he was, I hoped he would turn around so I could thank him, even if it was with a look or a smile. The class went normal, it was over and everyone left the room. Having the bouquet, I was a little late to put my things away.

"Did you... did you like them?" someone says from behind. I turned around and looked at him, he was a little distanced.

"Yes, thank you," I thanked sincerely.

He didn't say anything, just gave a nod and left.

I left school and found Rafa waiting in his car. I didn't expect it so it was a surprise to see it here. He approached me and he saw me a little confused by the bouquet.

"Hi, how did it go?"

"A little boring but okay, what are you doing here?"

"Well, I wanted to surprise my friend but I saw that someone else did it, nice bouquet," he says when he sees the roses, it was difficult not to see them, they are bright red.

"Thank you, I didn't expect them but I still liked them."

"A secret admirer?" He says as he opens my door and I get into the car, he goes around it and gets in.

"None of that, it was a... a classmate." He looks at me for a few seconds, waiting for me to say something else I guess but I have nothing else to say.

"Okay, well let's go to your house because your mom said we wouldn't be long because she will make green enchiladas."

"Yummy." I put on the seatbelt and looked at him again but he seemed to be staring at something outside. "Is something wrong?"

"Nothing, just, do you know who is looking here as if we were a threat?" I looked at him confused and then looked where he saw.

What is he doing here?!

Thiago was leaning against a tree in front of the school, he was looking here and you could easily see the anger and annoyance on his face. I saw how Brooke approached him and talked to him, the look towards us.

"It's no one, can we go?" He nods, not very convinced, and starts the car and we leave.

I know that in another situation I wouldn't worry about how he looked at us, I would just wonder why, but in this situation I do worry about how he looked at us.

I really wouldn't want to have to involve Rafa in this.

Chapter 35

JASMINE

February 14th arrived and my sister went out with Owen on a date. My dad brought a bouquet of flowers to my mom and she excitedly gave him a kiss, but not a simple one, it was one of those kisses that you rarely see parents give each other. It was nice to see that.

There were no classes today so I had the whole day to myself, my parents went out, my sister also went out and I... I have a date with someone called *Libro*, in my room with a coffee as a drink.

Who says I can't go on a date with myself?

It's past noon. I decided to take a bath before I could lock myself in my room. When I finish, I change and then I go to the kitchen and make my coffee; now ready, I go to my room and make myself comfortable.

"Should I watch a movie first or start reading?" What a difficult decision.

BROOKE

When I found out about the roses I was debating whether to send her a bouquet or not, after all this day not only belonged to lovers, but to friends, it is the day of love and friendship.

I didn't know if she was going to like them or if she was going to throw them in the trash. I was afraid of her reaction. Seeing her enter the classroom with the bouquet and a smile on her face made me feel happy and proud. I pretended to be asleep because I didn't quite dare to talk to her. After the... conversation we had, I'm afraid she'll reject me.

I had given me courage and I talked to her, and I was glad I did, I could see her smile. I know that partly she does it out of politeness, she doesn't want me to be part of her life, not in the near future.

When I left school I looked at Thiago leaning against one of the trees. It seemed strange to see him so I approached him and asked him what he was doing here. He just kept looking at a fixed point and I looked where he was, it was her with that guy.

I didn't understand the sudden approach, she had no friends apart from me and Thiago, after her trip was when I started seeing them together. I really didn't want to assume anything but yes, I was intrigued, what were they? her friend? a familiar? boyfriend?

But I was happy for her, but I knew that the one who was really bothered was Thiago, I know I didn't want to accept it but he really has an attachment problem towards Jasy.

"You have to calm down, tonight we have a job and if you don't calm down, it will be a problem."

"Calm down? Calm down?! How the hell do you want me to calm down knowing that that son of a bitch is with her all the damn time!"

"You don't know that," I said as I rubbed the bridge of my nose.

"Oh of course I know. You know better than anyone that I don't let anyone touch what's mine, after all, we went to the same school."

When I found out that Thiago was the problem child at my school I couldn't believe it, I was a child and didn't understand most things but it was a mere coincidence that we met again. The last I heard about that kid was that he was sent to the hospital and was no longer brought to school.

"Yes, they are together almost all the time but it does not mean that they are more than friends, what bothers you is that she is with him and not with you."

"*Besteria!*"

"English please."

"*Você não entende! Ela. É minha.*"

"Yes, I understand and no, she is not yours. Thiago, things are not always the way they are and stop saying that she is yours, she is a person, not an object."

"I know you don't understand it and you won't understand it but let me tell you something, human beings feel, all types of humans do it and I am not the exception, I like her, I love her or whatever, if you don't understand that then you are the one with the problem."

Thiago looks at me with a look full of fury. I know that a reasonable person would stop him from acting and thinking and I know that buried memory would do that but I don't want to go to extreme methods.

Well, almost extreme, the other thing would be to kill him but I'm not someone who plays with his own life.

I leave my room and go down to the kitchen to grab a bottle of water. I hear footsteps and he appears on the last step. I understand his point and about his obsession that he has with her—well, almost—but what worries me is that the guy who is with her is three or four years older than her. Thiago is only two years older.

"Go get your things, today we have to do something big if something goes wrong because of you, you are responsible." He rolls his eyes and goes up again.

Why do I feel like I just scolded a child?

I took my computer that was in the living room and put it in a backpack. Thiago arrives and we leave my house. The truth is I didn't think we had to work today, after all it's the fourteenth of February, it's not like I have anything good to do but who cares.

We got into my car and I started it. The whole way was silent, there was no word from either of us and that only bothered me more, I remembered that at times like this, Jasmine and I would be talking about whatever came to mind.

"Why the hell don't you do what I tell you?! See what you caused!"

"Don't blame me, you uncovered the wound and made the blood flow!"

"Motherfucker!"

We tried to put the body in the most credible position for an accident but with all the blood spread on the ground it clearly makes it look like a murder.

In the end we made it an act of revenge, after all, this bastard only did what he did for fun, surely there are many people who would like to hurt him.

When we finished, we left the house and everyone went their own way, it was night. I imagine that today no one thought about sleeping, not early at least. I had the intention of going home but I wanted to see how she was; I went out of my way and took another one. I don't know what I gained from this but I really wanted to know how she was doing or what she was doing.

I arrived at her house and almost all the lights were off, only two were on, I got out of the car and got a little closer. I stood in front of the window that was the brightest and through a small space given by the curtains I could see that it was the window of her room, she was lying down watching a movie with a cup in hand.

She looks comfortable, I'm glad.

I was about to leave but I heard the house bell ring, I looked at the time confused, it's almost ten at night, who would come so late? I got close enough to see the entrance, it was that idiot, her new "friend". Jasy opened the door and greeted him.

"Hi Rafa! What are you doing here?"

"I was just passing through, I went to the store and I thought I'd come check on you," he says as he lifts a bag.

"You shouldn't have, but I'm fine, I thought you were going out today."

"Why did you think that?" He smiles at her, I know he acts innocent and everything but I know he is interested in her.

There are many stores and I still don't know where he lives but I'm sure there is a store near his house and if he had to come by car that only tells me that he doesn't live in this neighborhood or this area. I still don't have the slightest idea how they met but I really would like to know, I know it's not something that matters to me but I can't help but not care about her.

She invited him inside... Jasmine, never do that if you're alone! My God!

I try to look through another window and I see them sitting in the living room, they seem to be talking but I don't hear anything. After a few minutes she seems to get excited and runs to her room,—or so I think. She comes back and stands in front of him.

She has something in her hands, she seems to have bags or something, I can't see clearly, and just when she is about to open one my phone starts to ring, I awkwardly try to take it out and turn it off but they heard me, they turned to me and I hid.

"Shit, Shit, Shit." I get away from there as fast as I can.

I get in my car and hide, I try to crouch down so that they can't see me from where they are. I see that they open the door and look everywhere; my heart is beating at full speed, I don't want her to recognize my car.

They go into the house and I let out a sigh. I look at my phone and see that it's Thiago.

Fuck you Thiago.

I called back but he didn't answer me. I'll send a message later. I stayed there for a few more minutes and then I left. I didn't want to leave her there but what else could I do, if she had discovered me it would be the end of me.

Chapter 36

JASMINE

Rafa left around twelve, we had put on masks and I had fun in the process. I thought that today I would spend it alone but the fact that he came just made my night.

I knew that the noise we heard was Brooke, it was the same tone as his phone, I thought maybe it was something else but when we went out to see what it was, I looked at his car parked a few meters from my house. Maybe that car belonged to someone else but only he would have a Canadian flag sticker on the front.

Rafa wanted to call the police to take a look but I convinced him not to, that it could have been a drunk person or an animal, something. We got into it and continued having fun. My parents had sent me a message saying they wouldn't be coming tonight—even parents have their "fun" moments alone—and Vanessa, well, I just hope a mini-her doesn't show up.

I didn't sleep all night, I stayed up watching movies and reading books that I hadn't read yet. There weren't many but they made me not think about other things for a long time. It's Thursday and I had classes.

I got ready, had a glass of milk with cookies and left the house. Along the way I only focused on thinking about what I want to do when I finish high school. The counselors are already on the heels of all the students and that is not pretty.

Should I continue studying like Vanessa? But what will I study? She is studying to be a lawyer but I don't want to do that.

I left the neighborhood and only had to cross a street, I waited until a car came and crossed. Several boys and girls carried gifts, chocolates, teddy bears, flowers and letters. The last time I received a letter was for a mandatory exchange when I was in elementary school, but it was a Christmas exchange.

"I just want to warn, for the seniors, that tomorrow there will be a meeting with you and your advisors, for those who already have a plan for later, there is no need to go," too bad, I'm not one of those. "Unless you want any advice or help. Students who still don't know what to do, need to go and are recommended to have at least a few schools to go to or if you plan to enlist in the military, air force or marines."

The class ended with that and we all left. It was the last class of the day and I already wanted to go home, I have homework but I don't even want to do that.

On the way, I looked at my mother's friend. She tried to cover me with my backpack but the woman recognized me.

"Jasmine! Dear, I'm Mrs. Martinez, your mom's friend." I have no choice but to greet her.

"Hola, Mrs. Martinez, what brings you here?"

"Well, I was going to the store to buy things for dinner. But hey, tell your mom that we agreed to eat, it wasn't possible when you returned from your trip but I'm looking forward to her visit," she says while smiling like when your *abuelita* makes you cookies.

"Yes, I'll tell her." What I will tell my mom is not to accept the invitation.

"Very well, *nos vemos querida*."

I got home and went straight to my room. I left my things on my bed and went out to look for my mom. I found her in the living room watching the afternoon novel.

"*Yo sabía que ella era una mendiga.*'

"*Ma*'" I spoke to her but she didn't answer me. "*Ama!*"

"*Que?*"

"Today, I saw your friend, please, whatever you want, don't go to her house. She insists and insists on going to dinner with them, but please, don't go!" I put both hands together and begged her.

"What are you talking about, *chiquilla*?"

"I know you don't believe me but she's up to something, *lo se*."

My mom completely ignores me, and she continues watching her novel.

I have nothing against that woman, she is a good person but she believes that I am "perfect" for her son. According to what I know, her son is about my age or a year older and I have never seen him. I don't understand how she came to that conclusion.

I wanted to snack on something so I took money and left the house. I was going to go to the store to see if there were any good things. Lately they only has oatmeal cookies but without sugar and those are not good.

My phone started to vibrate, while I was looking for it I wasn't looking where I was going, and when I took it out of my pocket I stopped suddenly when I saw a pair of shoes stop in front of me. That caused the phone to fall to the ground.

"*Chingado.*" I looked up and it was him.

He looked at me intensely, I didn't know what to do or what to say. I get away? It would be the most logical thing to do. I tried to go around him but he grabbed my arm, not forcefully but he stopped me. I didn't look at his face, I didn't dare to, I didn't want to be afraid of him but I really wanted to get away.

"We need to talk, I know you don't even want to see my face but please, please give me a chance, a chance to explain things," he says, sounding desperate.

"The thing is…"

"*Boneca*, I beg you."

I still didn't know what that word meant but every time he said it I felt a strange feeling, not bad but strange.

"You only say that, you keep saying things like: it's complicated, I can't tell you, you wouldn't understand it, *y no se que mas fregados.*"

I made him let go of my arm. He just looked at me, he looked at my eyes and I didn't look away. His hair is longer, before it was above his shoulders and now it is below.

"I know, fuck, I know, but I can't continue being without you."

"What are you talking about?" I was confused, I don't think that in that short time he had such a feeling.

"I know you don't remember but two years ago, two and a half years ago, I already knew you, I know that every afternoon during your second year of high school, you went to the store and bought those cinnamon cookies. I know you loved going to the library when you had time. I know you even stopped eating your favorite things because your self-esteem started to drop. And I know something that you don't, and you know what it is? That you are irresistible." At this point my heart was beating like crazy.

Did he just confess?

What was this? Did he already know me and know things about me when I barely noticed him? How do things work like this?

We were in the middle of the sidewalk and he was telling me all this. It felt like someone threw water at me out of nowhere and I didn't know how to react. Is it something good? Something bad? Should I be worried?

Everything in him radiated intensity. He felt what he said but, this is supposed to be something toxic? I wanted drama? Well here I have it.

Chapter 37

THIAGO

I told her, I finally told her. I didn't know how to feel, I know I've always wanted to tell her what I feel but telling her this means that she will distance herself from me more than she already is.

She was shocked. I understood it but I really wanted her to accept me.

"Say something please..." She lowers her gaze and I immediately hold her face.

"What do you want me to say?" she says quietly. "I'm glad you've been harassing me for two years? You do realize that with just this you can spend five to ten years in prison?"

Prison? Such a familiar place...

"I know that maybe you can't see it or even understand it because of how the situation is, but, I love you, I really do." Her gaze stood out and she looked me straight in the eyes. I couldn't tell if it was for impression, emotion or something else.

"What...?"

"I know it's not something you want to hear but I had to tell you, I needed to tell you." She didn't say anything and that made me nervous.

"To be honest, I don't know what to tell you."

"I know, I know you don't feel the same but..." I felt a little distressed, she was giving me a negative reaction. "I have a gift for you, it was supposed to be for Christmas and we don't have time for that anymore but I really wish you had it."

I handed her the bag and she took it with hesitation. I had taken out the bag from where I had kept it before. She opened it a little and when she looked at what was inside it she looked at me and immediately looked back at the bag. Jasmine took out the sweater and held it out to see it better.

"It's... it's cute…"

"I didn't know whether to give it to you because I was afraid you would reject it."

JASMINE

I was surprised, I didn't expect him to give me a gift. But he had to understand that, even if he gave me a gift or told me that he loves me, things can't be solved like that.

"Thiago, I appreciate it, but I don't understand what you expect from this." He just listens to me. "I decided that I can't continue with this, I really don't want to receive messages or calls saying things like this or saying that you will explain it to me or something like that. I want you and me to be at peace from today onwards and I'm sorry if this is making you feel bad but I just want peace."

After a few minutes he asks, "Are you dating him?"

"Who are you talking about?"

"Who am I talking about? The one who is always with you, the one who won't leave you alone, the one who keeps you away from me!" He's angry, he says things with pure anger.

"No, I don't go out with him, he's just my friend and if you expect me to tell you about him, you're very wrong." Knowing what he is makes me think about everything I know about murderers, the programs are not in vain.

"I just want to be with you, I want us to spend time together, I want to do all kinds of things with you Jasmine, *Boneca*."

"Stop calling me that, I don't know what it means but I don't want to be called by any other name than mine," I said, a little tired of this.

"What will happen to Brooke?"

"What will happen to him? Well, only he will know. I hope that in the future you are doing things that you can be proud of, and not this... goodbye Thiago and I mean it."

I turned around and went back on my way, my desire to eat something had disappe ared.

It's time to grow mentally. I know this will follow me until the end of my days but I can put it aside and continue with what I want to do without the two of them appearing out of nowhere.

I got home and went to my room lay down and looked at the ceiling. I looked at it for a few long minutes until it came to my mind what I want to do in life. I went to Vanessa's computer and looked for schools where they can give me the best for my career.

It was time for dinner, my mom was making the food while I was talking to my sister, I was telling her about what I wanted to do and she looked at me a little surprised and I understood her, it's not something I would surely be interested in. but it is not as if it were the unknown.

My dad came over and sat at the table, my mom served the food and when she finished setting the table she sat down with us and we started talking about how our day went.

"Ma, pa, I think I know that I want to study and before I tell you I want to say that it is something a little unusual coming from me." They saw each other then nodded.

"And what is it?"

"I want to be an architecture student. It's a career where you design houses and their structures, but not only houses, but also buildings and things like that." They looked at me with surprise.

They know that I spend my time drawing when I'm not reading or watching movies and I'm good at it. I feel like I'm very creative and, well, I hope I'm not wrong about this.

I always draw whenever I can, not always. Sometimes during classes or after classes.

Epilogue

People's lives can change from the top down. Sometimes the changes can be good or sometimes bad but it all depends on how one decides to continue with the decision already made. At first I didn't know what to do, I didn't know what to do about my life, I didn't know how I would do it when I finished high school, but in the end I decided that it was time to make a decision.

I met people who I thought would not harm my life but I was wrong and I had to cut ties with those people. I met someone who at first I thought he was just playing with me but over time I realized that he hurt everything

A few months had passed and now I was getting my things ready to go to university. My mom was about to cry as was my sister and my dad looked at me with pride and when I saw him I smiled.

My sister's boyfriend and Rafa were also here, he is the one who would take me to the airport, yes, I'm going out of state.

I knew that they were in the distance, they were watching me and as much as I wanted to say goodbye—at least to one of them—I couldn't, *era tiempo de borron y cuenta nueva.*

"*Te me cuidas okay,* and please call if you need anything, don't talk to weird strangers and…"

"Yes ma, I'm going to miss you too, but I'll come over the holidays."
She hugged me tightly and when she let go Vanessa hugged me.

"If you need help with something, call me, you know what I'm
talking about."

"Yeah."

I looked at my house one last time and got into the car. In the end
I couldn't resist it and looked back, there they were both. I could see
that one of them cut his hair and the other was the same, he stopped
going to school and from what I heard, he decided to finish school
online.

"Jasmine ready?" Rafa asks me.

"Yes, ready."

It's time to discover what awaits me in this other story, one where
this time I will be the protagonist.